Symphony

Lois Lamb

ISBN 978-1-63903-506-9 (paperback)
ISBN 978-1-63903-507-6 (digital)

Christian Faith Publishing, Inc.
832 Park Avenue
Meadville, PA 16335
www.christianfaithpublishing.com

Printed in the United States of America

To all of the women left to carry the load of life alone.

Prologue

Jade Kennedy-Barnes tossed and turned on the bed. The blankets were wet with her sweat. Once more, she dreamed of a semitrailer smashing into their car. She woke screaming. With trembling fingers, she reached over and turned on the bedside lamp, hoping to wipe the recurring dream from her mind in time to allow her to go back to sleep before going to the hospital and her nursing classes.

It had been several weeks since she had the dream that haunted her nights. It always started with her in a dim, dark place—where, she was never sure. All she could remember about the crash was the sudden blast of pain as the truck, with brakes screaming, crashed into their little car. She vaguely remembered seeing her small son's car seat flying by her seconds later, moments before she blacked out.

She had come in to the emergency room, still in a world controlled by her own pain. A nurse hung over her bed, trying to calm her as she struggled to get up. "Tommy? Where's my baby? Where is he?" she had screamed at the nurse.

"Lie still, dear. Your little boy is in another cubicle. Dr. Porter from Pediatrics is on his way to take care of him. In the meantime, you need to remain calm so we can get you assessed. Your husband is in the cubicle next to you."

"How is he?" she recalled asking.

"He's not doing very well, dear. We're doing the best we can."

"Tommy? How's Tommy?"

"I don't have a report on him yet. I believe someone said he has a head injury and a broken arm. I'll check for you."

The pain washed over her as she lay waiting to hear from Tommy. The noises from Ted's cubicle were frightening. Strange signs came from her left at times. She was only vaguely aware that the sounds stopped, and an eerie silence fell over the area. She had begged to be told what was happening. The nurses skirted her questions and advised her they were taking care of everything—she shouldn't worry.

Jade lay back on the bed. Her entire left hip area was on fire and her left wrist obviously broken. Even to the untrained eye, she knew the arm would never be quite the same again. She remembered having a fleeting thought about her future as a classical piano player. She remembered nurses hovering around her. An ER doctor strode into the tiny room, swishing the privacy curtain aside as he came. "What do we have here?" he asked in a loud irritating voice.

"She's got a broken arm, several cuts and bruises, and some bad looking areas in her left hip area," the nurse replied.

"Get her to X-ray right away. Add a CT of that pelvis. I'll see about an MRI later. Right now, I can see we need to get her into surgery right away. I think Dr. Patterson is done with his other orthopedic patient or will be soon. Catch him and tell him I need an assist on this one. I just hope we don't run into more serious internal injuries."

Jade barely heard what he was saying. She suffered moments of agony as three staff members moved her to a rolling gurney. "Please, can I see my baby? Where is he?" She saw one of the nurses give her a pitying look. What is wrong? Where's Tommy?

"We're doing our best for your baby. Just take it easy now. We need to get you taken care of."

"I want to see Tommy. I want to see my baby," she wailed as they rolled her out of the ER toward the X-ray department. From there, they took her straight to surgery. With no more say on where she went or what happened to her, she soon gave up and drifted into a drug induced coma before being sent to surgery. She knew no more for twelve hours.

She woke up to find her parents hovering over her bedside. She knew a lot of time had passed, or they could not have gotten there. As she came to, she realized her entire world had changed. Her husband, Ted Barnes, was dead; and she had to plan a funeral for him, a funeral she was unable to attend. Her two-year-old son was in a deep coma. She had injuries that required months of therapy and rehabilitation. Not only had her family changed, her chances of pursuing her music career and her financial situation had also changed. In the days of her recovery, she often relived the past three years over and over and over again.

There still remained many questions about the accident that left her life in limbo. She began to wonder if she would ever get her life under control again. While doing rehab exercises to help her walk again, she thought back over her life. How had she gotten to this place in her life?

Chapter 1

Jade Kennedy walked out of the music building at the university into a perfect summer day after practicing a classical piano piece for over an hour. She loved classical music and had planned a career with a University Symphony after she completed her senior concert the next semester. She was surprised to see Ted Barnes, a well-known figure on campus, waiting on the front steps. "Hi, pretty woman. Do you mind if I walk along with you?" he asked in his most charming way.

Jade wondered what possible reason Ted Barnes could have for greeting her. He was known mostly as a good timer who flirted with every skirt that walked by. She wondered what he was doing here and why he was targeting her. "No, go ahead if you'd like. I was just heading for the Union for something to drink."

"I'd like to tag along." He grinned.

She looked at him out of the corner of her eye as they walked along. He was a handsome figure. His thick brown hair and sky-blue eyes, along with a physique gained from hours in the gym, caught the eye of most of the girls on campus. He was always dressed like a male model and could be found at almost every social event on campus. He had been elected senior class president the spring before and was ready to graduate in business administration in May. Jade knew he was popular with the ladies. It was considered an honor to be seen in his company.

She wondered what he wanted with her. She had little money, a few wellworn clothes, and another year of classes. She couldn't imagine why he was walking with her to the Union. She knew they would be seen and discussed all over campus by evening. She was hot and tired and really didn't care who was with her. All she wanted was a cool drink. It would be nice to have someone to visit with for a few minutes at least.

At the Union, Ted ordered drinks for them and led her to a table for two in a far corner. Several female students watched him with envy in their eyes when they saw Jade sitting down with him. "Did you notice those girls watching us?" he asked as he set the drinks on the table. "I'll bet they are jealous of me. You are so beautiful, Jade. That mass of curly hair is enough to drive a man crazy, and your eyes are beautiful." He reached across the table and took a lock of her hair in his hand. He twisted it around his finger before releasing it. Jade was amazed that she reacted to the simple gesture as much as she did.

Jade answered him self-consciously, "I thank you, but I'm just a plain coed trying to get through school. I don't think much of my looks. I just want to get through college and start making money instead of spending it."

They chatted over the drinks. An hour later, Ted looked at his watch and announced, "I have another meeting in twenty minutes. I'd really like to see more of you. Would you consider going out for dinner with me tonight?"

Later Jade had wondered why she had suddenly been so eager to say yes to his invitation. She knew she had a ton of studying to do for an advanced Music History class the next day. It was the one elective she had chosen to complete her major requirements. Most of the material was familiar to her, but she wanted to review everything one more time. She would get her degree after completing a senior concert with the University Symphony.

"Come on, Jade. Don't break my heart. I just want to spend more time with you." She didn't see him give the "thumbs-up" sign to the group of men sitting at a table near the window. Later he would tell her he had asked her on a bet with them. The group had watched her routines for days and bet him that she would not go out with him. Later he would tell her, "It was a game, Jade. We picked out the prettiest women on campus and tried to see who could get a date with her first. It was just a game."

"That's awful, Ted. You only pick the prettiest girls, use them, and then dump them."

"Don't be a prude, Jade. It's something fun to do."

"What about your classes?" she had asked him.

"Classes? Oh, I never go to classes. My parents donate a lot of money to the U, so I don't have to do a lot of studying. A 'D' will pass me close enough."

Jade had been overwhelmed by his initial attention. She had no family left but a distant aunt who had always encouraged Jade in her music study. Looking back on the courtship, Jade wondered if she had just been terribly lonely since the death of her parents—her mother to Cancer and her dad to suicide shortly after her mother's death—when she was fifteen.

That first dinner had been nice. Ted was polite and charming. He asked her to go to a football spring practice with him the next Saturday. She wasn't a fan of football other than to urge them on if they happened to be on television. The reality of thousands of screaming people confined to the stadium was more than she could stand. And talking about stand, at five foot four, you could literally stand and still not see the game. For her, the one game she had attended her freshman year had been a miserable experience of attempting to see the field while dodging spilled beer and coeds passed overhead to the top of the stadium. She had finally sat down and reviewed notes in her head while the crowd around her had yelled and stomped in unison as she assumed someone had scored. She vowed never to attend another game. Even the replay cameras and screens were hard for her to see.

Ted had been an avid fan of the team. She reluctantly agreed to go to the spring training the next Saturday. It turned out to be a little more tolerable than an actual game. There were only a few hundred spectators and none of the drunken, screaming fans she had disliked at the fall game. Ted continued to introduce her proudly to coaches and players. He seemed to be in his social element just being around the group of men. Jade had joined a small group of women who chatted about "girly" things while the men watched the team line up against each other for the exhibition game.

He asked her to marry him the first time following the game. She had turned him down stating that she wanted to finish her degree the next year before she even considered entering into a marriage that would curtail her music dreams. "It's way too soon for us, Ted. I may consider in a couple of years. I will keep seeing you, but I won't get married now. I want to finish my degree and travel with the Symphony for at least one year."

"Just think, Jade. My folks have plenty of money. They would be glad to see me settled down." He failed to mention that his dad had threatened to cut him off completely if he didn't raise his grades and finish college after six years on campus. "Mom always says I'm too flighty. They want me to find someone and quit having so much fun. I've got news for them. It will be a long time before I settle down like they want. They are a couple of stuffy social climbers."

They had gone together for a month before Ted began to complain about her dedication to her studies. "Come on, Jade. Have a little fun with me." He had run his hand up the back of her arm. Even through the thin blouse, she could feel the heat of his hand. She had felt no particular desire created by the touch. "So what if you miss a note on that piano you play? Life is too short to be a stick-in-the-mud all the time."

She told herself it was foolish to waste so much time playing at his games. Bars turned out to be as foreign to her as the football games. She ignored her own feelings and joined Ted and his buddies at the bar. He had told her that he had fallen madly in love with her and that if she loved him, she would show him. He pushed for sex on every date. She continued to resist, stating that she simply was not ready to take on a husband at that stage of her education.

She was never quite sure what had happened that Friday night when they had been going together for three months. She remembered feeling a little strange right after she told Ted she was ready to go home. Later she would wake up in a motel room with Ted asleep beside her. She had been horrified until Ted reassured her by saying they were married. He produced a marriage certificate from a nearby state where no waiting periods were in effect. She knew she would never have agreed to the wedding if she had been coherent. Ted had surely laced her drink with the "date rape" drug. She was trapped for the time being. Her music studies, her part-time job in the library, and her other classes took a great deal of her time. The first time she realized that Ted was as extravagant at spending money as he was at partying was when her paycheck disappeared from her purse. When she asked about it, he made some excuse about needing it to pay a debt.

"Dad and Mom provide all I want. They were getting tired of paying some of my bills. They think now that I'm married, things will get better. I've got news for you. I intend to keep having fun."

Within a month, Ted came home telling Jade about a really hot chick he had seen at the Union. She began to suspect he was still playing the game with his friends. At that time, she assumed it was one of the other guys who would be approaching the pretty girl asking for a date.

Jade was dismayed to find that she was pregnant six weeks after the wedding. She realized it when she suffered the first morning sickness—a sickness that would last until the baby was born. Ted had not taken it well. "You bitch, I never wanted kids. They are just a burden. I'll tell you right now, you can raise it on your own. The folks will up the money for expenses, but don't plan on me for help. I don't intend to change. I'm having too much fun."

She had begun to see him for what he really was, a spoiled brat who cared nothing for others. Life was a game for Ted, one where he could play as he pleased. He had married her because he needed a wife to hide behind. The pretense of the union became more apparent the longer they were married. The good job he had gotten with the Sports Department at the university lasted only three months. They fired him on the grounds of underperformance after he failed to report to work several days following his late-night parties. Jade knew she was caught in a bad situation. She vowed to have the baby, find someone to sit with it, and go back to finish her degree as soon as possible. In the meantime, she couldn't see herself asking the Barneses for money to divorce their playboy son.

The baby was born on a hot August morning. They had taken their son, Thomas James Barnes, home when he was twenty-four hours old. The first six months he suffered from colic. Jade had been relieved to be over the constant vomiting while she carried him, but she was not prepared for the days and nights of sleeplessness that plagued those first months. Ted spent little very time at their apartment and soon developed a habit of "staying over" with the guys so he could get some sleep. Several times he had tried to get her to go to the bar with him, but she declined because of the baby. When the semester began, she put off enrolling because of Tommy's colic and her extreme exhaustion. In her mind, she knew she could finish her degree another time.

She had returned to the Music Building to show them Tommy when he was three months old. He was a darling baby with a big smile he had just learned to give anyone who talked to him. "He's a beautiful baby," Professor Taylor told her. "Have you found someone to keep him while you come back to school?"

"Not really, he may be darling now, but in the middle of the night, when he is screaming, he's not so cute. I simply can't leave him and continue my studies. I'm so exhausted all the time. I can't get away when I need hours and hours to get ready for a concert. Will I be able to come back in another semester and finish my degree?"

"Of course, as long as you make sure you keep practicing in the meantime. Now you go home and try to get some sleep. They always tell me that the first two years of a baby's life are the best. Enjoy him."

"Enjoy him" rang through her ears. Yes, she did enjoy Tommy. It was just that Ted did not pay any attention to him and came home later and later, or didn't come home at all. She heard some coeds talking in the mall one day while shopping for clothes for Tommy. "Carrie is devastated. He was so charming. He gave her the bum's rush and then told her he's married. I'm really worried about her. She may commit suicide over this." They walked on down the center atrium so Jade did not hear the other girl's reply.

Jade didn't think anything about the conversation until she saw an obituary in the paper the next week. The girl's first name was Carrie. She had been found dead in her bed from an overdose of sleeping pills. There was a picture of a laughing beautiful girl at a sports event. Jade turned cold when she recognized Ted standing next to her with his pals grinning in the background. She sensed that they had been involved some way with the dead coed.

She fretted a few days before asking Ted if he had known the girl. He commented casually, "I don't think I've ever heard of her. Too bad, she obviously couldn't handle real life." She held out the paper with the picture.

Defensively, he told her, "I don't know how they got that picture. I did go to that event, but I don't know her." Jade sensed he was lying, but she didn't challenge him at that time. She began to ask herself if she really cared anymore.

Time flew by, and Tommy approached two years old. Jade had still not felt comfortable enough to leave Tommy to get her degree. She had taken a job at the university as a secretary to the head of Women's Studies. She enjoyed the job and constantly learned about the status of women worldwide and in the state. Secretly, she hoped to take the classes offered to their employees, but Ted still complained about her silly dreams of finishing her education.

On a beautiful spring day, they left the house on one of the few occasions they went out together. There was a picnic planned by a group of Ted's buddies at a state park east of town. Ted had put Tommy's car seat in his car after removing it from Jade's and carried her vegetable casserole to the car in a picnic basket along with paper plates, plastic silverware, and Tommy's favorite snacks.

Ted was in a particularly bad mood that day. He had been reprimanded by the company boss the day before because of the number of missed days and late check-in times. "Those dumb bastards, they think they own a guy's time. I was never more than thirty minutes late. It seems too early to be there anyway. I'd rather work from nine to six than eight to five."

Jade hadn't said anything as he drove toward Interstate 80. When he pulled on the highway, he soon began to curse at the traffic. Tommy began to cry. Jade's nerves were on edge. "Oh, Ted, it will be all right. Let's just go to the picnic and have a good time." That was the last Jade remembered about the drive.

She came to in an Emergency Room cubicle sometime later. She could hear medical workers in the next room snapping orders. She was in such pain. Her entire left side was on fire from the waist down, and her left arm was killing her. She felt blood on her face and arms. She heard herself moaning as people moved her around.

Ted, she vaguely remembered his anger and his cursing the traffic. She heard a voice calling for blood typing from Ted's cubicle. "Get me some O positive. I can't wait for typing, or this guy isn't going to make it."

A nurse hurried by with a bag of dark blood in her hand. What seemed like hours later, Jade heard horrible gagging sounds coming from Ted. She heard someone call frantically, "Get me a trach set. This guy can't breathe." The noises continued and then stopped abruptly. She heard unfamiliar noises of people coming and going before a male voice said what seemed an eternity later, "Never mind, this guy's dead. I need to see to the child."

Jade tried to struggle off the bed, but the pain was too intense, and her left leg refused to cooperate with her. "Tommy?" she screamed. "Where's my little boy?"

A nurse gently pushed her back. "Just lie down, dear. You will be fine. We are taking you to X-ray. You have a broken left wrist, and we think a broken hip or pelvis. Your little boy is in cubicle 6."

Jade had sensed the total silence coming for that area. Jade vaguely remembered telling them to do everything they could to save him as they rolled her away to X-ray and surgery. She heard the nurse say as they rolled her by, "His car seat wasn't fastened properly. It came loose and let him hit the dash. He has head injuries. He's in a coma now."

"Save him please, save him," Jade begged through a haze of pain.

"We'll do our best. Now we're going to take care of you." She remembered the final question, "Do you have insurance?"

Chapter 2

The next weeks were a blur. Tommy remained unresponsive in his coma when Jade came out of surgery. They
placed a feeding tube in his chest to feed him a liquid diet.
His left arm had been broken. "He'll probably come around
in a day or two," one of the Pediatric Doctors told her.

The first time Jade had been able to make the trip from
Orthopedics to Pediatric had been torture for her. Not only
was she in extreme pain from her own injuries, she nearly
broke down when she saw her beautiful little boy lying so
still in the big white hospital bed. After that first time, she
had insisted on being rolled to his bed every day to sing
to him, read to him, and to play tapes of her playing the
piano. She remembered that Tommy liked to hear her play
on the tiny keyboard she had in the apartment.

Months passed as she rehabilitated and Tommy continued to lie very still, unresponsive to outside stimuli. He
remained away from her in a world only he could know.
The Head of Pediatrics, Dr. Porter, informed her she might
as well quit coming so often as there was no progress. She
heard him tell the nurse who accompanied him on rounds,
"I don't know why they even saved that kid. I can't see any
hope for him except to keep running up bills."

All they're doing is running up bills. Is that all my baby means to him? He's got to come around. I don't know how I can go on if he doesn't. If I had known he was going to be like this, would I have made the same decision in the ER? I was so scared for him and hurting so much at that time. I had just heard Ted die. I didn't want to lose my baby too. I'm not so sure about Ted. I think I am better off that he died. Planning a funeral from a hospital bed while you are doped up on high-powered drugs was one of the first things I faced. She remembered making decisions about Ted's burial after his parents, Harold and Clarice Barnes, had come to the hospital and advised her that they would no longer help with bills.

Clarice claimed to be devastated by the loss of her only son. They had found Jade sitting in a wheelchair by Tommy's bed two weeks after the accident. They had merely glanced at Tommy before informing her that they were in no way responsible for their son's funeral expenses or the medical bills for Tommy. Harold had hinted that they thought she had been somehow responsible for the accident. She hated the thought that she couldn't remember the details. There were moments when she knew they had been going to a picnic, but she couldn't remember what had happened during the time that led up to Ted pulling into the oncoming lane to pass a slower vehicle and meeting the semi head-on. In the back of her mind was the niggling little thought that she had somehow caused Ted to swerve at that moment, a moment that cost him his life and Tommy's consciousness. It would not have been unusual for them to have been fighting over something. She didn't bother to consider at that time how much her own life had been changed.

She had been relieved to see the Barneses leave but couldn't believe the conversation she overheard in the hallway. "Dr. Porter, I see you are the Head of Pediatrics," Harold was saying. "We are the Barneses. Tommy is our grandson. Has he made any response to you?"

Porter answered quietly, "I don't see much progress. The scans don't show any permanent damage, but he hasn't come around for two weeks. It doesn't look good to me. I am thinking he is going to be a vegetable. Perhaps if his mother had let him go in ER, the kid would be better off. He could lay there for years running up enormous hospital bills for the state. I doubt the mother has enough money to keep him here forever."

"I'm sure she doesn't. We have been supplementing our son's income, but I have no intention of supporting her or her vegetable any longer."

As their voices faded down the hallway, Jade had rolled her wheelchair back to Tommy's bedside and stared at him. He was so beautiful lying there, but there was no sign of the busy little boy he had been before the accident. She remembered fun days when she chased after the busy little boy. One day, she had caught him sitting in the middle of the kitchen table as proud as could be—an hour later he was playing in the bathroom stool, another hour found him in the toy box with all of the toys scattered around him. He stole her heart with a big toothy grin and big blue eyes.

Tommy had just begun to try new words before the accident. She had worried about his lack of interest in talking until she learned in a psychology class that children often didn't talk until they were nearly forced to. Perhaps she had spoiled him too much, but he was so sweet. As she remembered, she laid her head on his bed and cried for what seemed like the hundredth time.

An hour later, a nurse found her still sitting by the bed. "Are you ready to go back to your room?" she asked Jade.

"Yes, I have to be in therapy at 3:00, and I have some other things to plan while I'm there." Back in the room, Jade sat staring out the window. In the back of her mind, she must have thought that the Barneses would step forward and help her with Tommy even though they didn't approve of her. She was truly on her own from that moment on. Sadly she admitted she needed to go on welfare as soon as she was released. The health insurance Ted had in force would pay for Tommy's expenses for a long time if she could pay the premiums. She wondered if there was a limit on what they would pay. She'd have to face that hurdle when she came to it.

At that time, she needed to get well herself. She had no idea what she would do. Music had been her life and the piano her instrument. The broken left wrist was healing nicely, but she could tell it was definitely weaker and often ached when she tried to do the rehabilitation exercises. She would have to make up her mind to do something else other than music, a career where she could earn a salary big enough to keep herself near Tommy.

As she visited Tommy every day, she noticed a middle-aged nurse at the main desk every week day. One afternoon, the nurse came down the hall and asked if she would care to join a group of nurses in the lounge to celebrate one of their birthdays. Jade had accepted, grateful for the opportunity to do something pleasant for a change. She was soon drawn to the older woman. They became friends as Jade came to the department every day. Her name was Maggie Hill.

They soon made a habit of having coffee in the nurse's lounge each weekday afternoon. "So how's Tommy today?" Maggie always asked first.

The usual answer was "The same. He doesn't move much. Once in a great while, he moves an arm or a leg like he was uncomfortable. I guess it's the stillness that bothers me the most. He used to be so busy. He just lies there like a doll. I wish I knew if he thinks or feels anything."

"Keep the faith, girl. Movements like that are usually a sign that he may be coming out of it. He'll surely come around soon. In the meantime, I see that you are doing some walking with crutches. How are you getting along?"

She laughed. "Oh, Maggie, I'm worse than a baby trying to walk. I use the crutches a lot in my room. They tell me I have to find something to do with myself before long. They plan to kick me out of the hospital as soon as I can manipulate the crutches or a walker." She sighed. "I just wish I knew what I was going to do when I get out. I can come to the hospital, but I don't know what kind of work I can do. I do have some money left over from the car insurance company. Once it's gone, I'll have to find work and a career where I can at least keep myself."

"Have you ever thought about the nursing career? I watch you with Tommy. You're a natural nurse. The program doesn't start for two more months, but you should apply now. I'll be happy to recommend you if you'd like."

"I do admire you, girls. Lisa and you have done so much for Tommy. I don't think I could do what the aides do, but if I trained, I should be able to be a nurse. I'll get the brochures and see how much of my previous work will transfer to the Nursing Program. I just hope I can pass the science classes."

Maggie, Lisa, and Jade poured over leaflets and course requirements the next few days. She talked to the Registrar's Office to see how much work she could transfer. The next day, she swung into the lounge on her crutches at coffee time. "Guess what, girls? I can enter the nursing program as a third-year student. I just found out that the anatomy and human physiology classes I took will help fulfill the nursing prerequisites. I only need another biology class and two chemistry classes to satisfy all of the prereqs. I can do the biology class online starting now and consider doing the first chem class over the summer. They even advised me to talk with the head of the department, but they think I should be accepted under the circumstances. There is always a student or two that drops out, leaving openings each year."

Maggie jumped up and hugged her. "Congratulations. I am going to take the credit for recruiting you to the profession. We will all be glad to help you, well, most of us will. Lisa and I aren't so sure about Penny Hansen. She's a third year student too, but nobody likes her much. She shirks her duties whenever possible. She's on the night shift right now. She's even been caught sleeping in one of the empty rooms. That dumps more work on the others. I'm not sure she's really good to the patients either. Too many little ones end up crying after she leaves a room."

"I think she smacked one of the kids who had a badly broken shoulder when he didn't do what she wanted him to. I don't think she knew I was there. I didn't actually see her do it, but it sounded like a slap to me. The little boy cried for a long time afterward," Lisa told them.

"I had better never catch her hitting Tommy," Jade told her.

"He just lies there. No one could accuse him of causing trouble," Maggie added.

"I know. You can't imagine how many times I've wished he'd wake up and throw something at me like he used to when he was playing. What little he does move hasn't changed much over the last two months." Tears filled Jade's eyes. "I miss those days so much. If I don't keep busy, I'll just sit around and feel sorry for myself."

Chapter 3

They dismissed Jade from the hospital in late June. She found a note on Fifth-floor bulletin board looking for a roommate to a nursing student. She called the number to see what Lori Brewster was offering.

"I have a two-bedroom in a large apartment complex. I've been here with an older student for two years, but now I need someone to share expenses for the next year and a half at least. I'll be glad to show you the extra bedroom if you'd like. I live just about a mile from the hospital. There is a bus every fifteen minutes that I use to get back and forth."

Jade told her, "Tell me which bus to take, and I'll be there to look at the room right now. How much do you need for rent?"

"It's only three hundred each plus utilities around three hundred more to split on top of that. It's not the most desirable complex in town, but the apartment is adequate for a student, and it's close to the hospital. I'll come down to the bus stop and meet you."

"I'll be the one on crutches." Jade laughed. "I'll catch the next one coming that way."

Jade managed to load on the bus ten minutes later. She had already gone halfway through the two-block-long building when her hip and pelvis began to ache from the strain of walking the long distance on marble floors. She knew she would have to do more physical therapy in order to stand up to the nurse's training program in two months.

They had dismissed her two weeks later. She was thankful that Lori and she had hit it off immediately. It was one of those friendships that you know you will keep forever. When she arrived at the apartment, she thought about the house where she and Ted had lived. His parents had paid for it, so they had been responsible for the house after Ted died. Bitterly, Jade thought about her possessions at the house. She would have to contact Clarice to see where her things were. In the meantime, she settled into the second bedroom.

The next morning, she dialed Clarice's number. Harold answered the phone, "Hello."

"Harold, this is Jade."

"What do you want? I told you I didn't intend to support you and that kid."

Jade took a deep breath to keep from screaming at him. "I'm calling to find out what you have done with my things from the house."

"You'll have to talk to Clarice about that. We have cleaned out the house to sell it. It was in our name after all," he explained defensively. "Clarice was going to pack up anything that was yours. She can tell you how to get them."

Clarice answered the phone several minutes later. *She's letting me know how unimportant I am by making me wait. Just as soon as I get my stuff, I hope I never have to see either one of them again.* Clarice answered sweetly, "Hello, dear. Harold tells me you're looking for things from the house. I have your clothes packed for you. I didn't really see anything else that you would want.

Just my computer, my files, and the blanket and vase that belonged to my mother. "What about my computer?"

"Oh, was that yours? I gave it to the used store down the street. There was a nice little file cabinet full of useless looking files so I had them burned. If you wanted them, I'm sorry."

Sorry. I'll bet you are. I'll show you. I'll make it without any help from you. I'll have to buy a computer right away for my classes. The files held all my college work and my birth certificate. I'll have to order a new one right away. I heard that will cost $20. I need a better job.

She told Maggie about going after her clothes. "They were in a couple of boxes in their basement. That was the only thing she had packed. She donated everything else, even the kitchen items, to the used store. I'm sure they're gone."

"I'll be done in five minutes. Let's drive over to the used store and see if any of your items still there. Some things don't turn over very fast, especially odds and ends."

"That's a great idea. I didn't think of that. I'll be glad to wait for you." They met twenty minutes later.

As they started out the door, Maggie called, "Oops. I forgot my keys to the medicine safe. Give me one minute, and I'll be ready."

Ten minutes later, the two of them walked into the used store. As she wandered through, Jade spied the old red-glass vase that had been her grandmother's. She picked it up. With tears in her eyes, she showed Maggie. "This belonged to my mom's mom. I always loved the red glass. They have a quarter on it. It's worth a million to me to have it back. I hope there is something else here."

A few minutes later, she spotted her mother's blanket hanging on a hanger with some bedspreads and sheet sets. She assumed it hadn't been sold because the weather was too warm. In a few months, someone would have snapped it up. In the kitchen department, she found a couple of her mother's old casserole dishes. No one wanted Corning Ware anymore, but she loved them.

She spotted her file cabinet in another area. Unfortunately, it was empty, just as Clarice had said it would be. She and Maggie struggled to load the file cabinet in the trunk of the car. Jade was elated to have a small pile of things that had been her mother's. The matching set of china her mother used for special occasions had been marked $10, and one of the old cast-iron skillets her mom had used to fry chicken were in the kitchen area. She knew she would have paid much more just to have those things back. "Oh, Maggie, I can't tell you how happy I am you thought to do this. It cost me a total of $18, but I at least retrieved some of my things. I can't thank you enough."

Back at the apartment, she folded the blanket across the foot of her bed and set the red vase where the morning sun would shine on it. She knew it would make a red halo across the wall as it reflected the sun. "I have everything put away. I suppose the computer sold right away. I can't believe she would donate it. Clarice had to know I used the computer."

Lori sympathized with her. "It sounds like a spite thing to me."

"Maybe I can find some other things I need at the used store. The clerk told me they get all kinds of electronics in as soon as summer school ends in three weeks. I can use the library computers until I find something," she told Lori that evening.

The clerk had told her, "A lot of people come here for special workshops and buy a setup when they get here and donate it when they leave. The Writer's Workshop is famous for that. If you'll leave me your name and number, I'll call you is something reasonable comes in August."

The next day, she told Maggie, "I'll take another trip out there before I spend much money on a computer and printer."

In August, she received three phone calls the first week. The first advised her that she was completely enrolled in the nursing program. She was to report for her first class in two weeks. She barely had time to celebrate her acceptance before the used-store clerk called her to tell her someone had just donated a great laptop with a printer. She drove Lori's car to the store a few minutes later. The computer was like new. Whoever had donated it had included a great laser printer and three reams of good quality paper. She purchased the entire setup for $175.

The third call came from the hospital informing her that they would be happy to give her a part-time job in the Business Department of the hospital. She was to start immediately.

"I can't think of another thing I need," she told Maggie the next afternoon when she visited Tommy's room, "unless it would be for Tommy to wake up. Dr. Porter doesn't think there's much chance of improvement, but I keep hoping."

Maggie picked up Tommy's chart from the hanging file. "I see that Penny Hansen is reporting that Tommy is moving around a lot at night. I heard her say it gave her the creeps when he moved. I don't know what that indicates. Porter thinks it's nothing, but I wonder. You might want to see if you can detect any change. I did think I saw him moving around yesterday."

"I certainly hope so. I'm not surprised to hear he moves more at night. He kept me up almost every night the first year and a half after he was born."

Jade's first year in the nursing program had flown by. She found that she loved the work. By the end of her second semester in the program, she quit her job in the business office and took one in the Pediatrics department, assisting with paperwork. She was able to spend a lot of time with Tommy. Other than increasing restlessness on rare occasions, there was no sign of improvement in his condition. Dr. Porter seldom visited his room. Jade felt that he considered Tommy a hopeless case, a burden on society.

That same year, word came down from the hospital administrator that Dr. Porter had asked for early retirement from Head of Pediatrics even though he was only sixty. They announced that they would be searching for a new Head of Pediatrics immediately. Everyone anxiously awaited the decision of who to hire. Some wanted an internal doctor, and others thought they should advertise nationwide. The board met and decided that they would do a nationwide search. They should draw someone with perfect credentials for the hospital who was wellknown throughout the country. The Head of Pediatrics there would be an honor for someone.

In late July, they announced that they had hired Dr. Jeffrey Davidson as the new Head of Pediatrics. He was coming to them from Oklahoma University. They advised he was a skilled surgeon, as well as a teaching professor, specializing in Medical Ethics. Jade read his credentials and decided to enroll in the class. It would be an elective for her, but it sounded like a good offering. Jade hoped that the new head would bring some new ideas for Tommy's treatment. She thought no more about it as she went to work and prepared to begin her third semester in nursing.

The day of her first round of classes the first semester of her senior year, Jade slipped into Tommy's room an hour and a half before the Medical Ethics class was to begin. She nodded to the night nurse before heading toward room 512. As she walked through the door, she noticed the silence. The fragile-looking five-year-old boy lay on the hospital bed in a coma. She tiptoed past the bed and searched the nightstand in the half dark of early morning until she found a stack of discs in the drawer and set one in the CD player on the dresser. Classical piano music filled the room when she pressed play. She stood beside the bed looking at the little boy who lay there. Tommy Barnes looked like an angel. His soft brown hair had been buzzed for easier care. She remembered how his big blue eyes, so much like her own, had twinkled with mischief before the accident that left him in the hospital bed. She edged around the bed and sat down in the recliner. She popped her feet up and leaned back to listen to the haunting strains of one of her favorite compositions. Inevitably her mind drifted back to the day of the accident. Tommy had been all that held her failing marriage together.

Once again, she reviewed the past. Jade had been a fourth-year student in music at the university when Ted Barnes blew into her life. Her career as a classical pianist had taken second place to his charming ways. She only needed to finish the first semester and one final semester to complete two classes and perform a senior recital with the university orchestra to gain her degree.

Academically her life was right on track until Ted Barnes appeared into her life and turned it into chaos. She received the bum's rush by the charming, well-todo computer technologist. Often, she tried to remember the night of their marriage. It angered her to know that Ted had put something in her drink to get her to agree to his wishes. She remembered hours of screaming laughter with a group of his friends before the partygoers had dispersed to go their separate ways. Jade recalled waking up in a motel room with Ted passed out beside her. There had been empty liquor bottles on the table along with a marriage certificate stating that Kathleen Jade Kennedy and Theodore James Barnes had been married early that morning in a "no wait" state. The certificate looked legal enough to be real.

To her dismay, it was real. She had been mildly happy about it at the time. After all, Ted had promised her a great life with him days before the party. Surely it would be the beginning of a perfect life together. Jade knew within three days that she had made mistake number one.

She still had in mind finishing her classes after the marriage. Ted's constant neediness for her attention soon monopolized her time. She was required to go with him while he partied until the early morning hours. She could barely drag herself out of bed to attend early morning classes. By the end of the next semester, one semester away from attaining her degree in Performing Arts, Ted simply demanded that she give up her dream of a music career and be his wife.

When she found out about the pregnancy six weeks after the marriage, she was stunned but still considered that she would finish her senior year and delay her career with the Symphony. She didn't count on the morning sickness that lasted all day. It soon depleted what strength she had in reserve. She was so sick over the first two weeks of January that she had to drop out of school and delay her last semester of work. Ted was irritated at the thought of a baby and angry that she was sick all the time.

"I didn't get married to watch my wife barf all day," he ranted. "Now you're going to have a kid that I don't want. Babies droll and cry and stink. I remember my little sister. What a pain in the ass. You know you will be responsible for the kid if you chose to keep it. I'd prefer you didn't. I can get you the help to get rid of it." There had been no question in Jade's mind. She would keep the baby even though she knew Ted considered Tommy her mistake.

Tommy had been born on a blazing hot August day while Ted was playing pool at a local bar. She had called him to tell him she needed to go to the hospital. He told her, "Call a cab. I'll be there when my games are over." Her labor had gone relatively easy after the months of continual nausea. Tommy had been a perfect eight-pound-two-ounce infant. She had named him Thomas James after her grandfather and Ted. Ted had shown up the next day at three to take her to the small house his parents had purchased for Ted near the campus. He explained his absence by telling her he was having too good a time to stop and he had no need to go home if she wasn't there to feed him. He had shown no interest in his son. As much as she hoped that would change, it had not.

Mistake number three had been to stay with Ted as long as she did. She had thought that Ted's parents would be proud of their grandson, but they refused to acknowledge the marriage or the child. They had plenty of money but vowed to spend nothing on "that woman and her brat."

Chapter 4

Jade shifted in the chair as the disk wound down. She glanced at the clock. *Damn. I spent too much time here. Now I have to hurry, or I'll be late for the first day of my Medical Ethics classes. I only have twenty minutes to get to the auditorium nearly two blocks across the hospital.* She jumped up, kissed her son, and grabbed her class papers before rushing out the door.

She rammed head-on into a tall dark-haired man striding down the hall. Both Jade and her papers went flying to the floor, and his plastic clipboard flew out of his hand to land on the marble floor, breaking in two and scattering his papers among hers. "What the hell? Watch where you are going, lady," he yelled at her.

From the floor, Jade apologized, "I'm so sorry. I was distracted." She bent awkwardly to retrieve her papers. As he leaned down to help her retrieve the papers, Jade peeked at the stranger. *Oh my, he is a gorgeous hunk of man. Those eyes are so dark blue they look black.* They reached for some of the papers at the same time. Their hands brushed. Jade nearly jumped back as a mild shock ran up her arm. She was aware that he looked sharply at her a moment before taking several papers from her.

Jeffrey Davidson, MD, was furious to be delayed getting to his class. He was surprised when a pair of the biggest sky-blue eyes he had seen stared at him for a long second before long dark lashes swept down over them, hiding the look of extreme sadness shining there. "Here, give me some of those," he said gruffly as he grabbed papers out of her hand. He glanced at the broken clipboard before searching through the pile for his notes.

She had time to register that he wore a white doctor's coat over jeans and a plaid cowboy shirt with snaps and cowboy boots. *Cowboy boots in a hospital! In a hospital! All he needed was a hat to go with the boots, and he would look more like a bull rider than the doctor the longer white coat indicated he was.* She thought that a little odd as she hurried to gather the last of the papers.

She sat on the floor and sorted them as quickly as possible. *This is taking way too much time. Now I'll have to almost run to the auditorium. I'm not sure how my hip will take it if I have to run to get there.* The strange doctor snatched the last of his papers, gave her a cold glare, and abruptly stalked off down the hall, leaving the broken clipboard and Jade sitting in the hallway.

Jade finished sorting her papers as quickly as she could, bent awkwardly to pick up the clipboard, and glanced down the hall after the retreating figure. *First, I'm late, and then I lose time with a total jerk. Now I have to hurry, or I'll never make the lecture in time.* It was a struggle for her to gain her feet. The broken hip had healed nicely, but it still gave her problems if she stood too long or walked too far. She assessed herself carefully. She had landed on her right side, protecting the injured left side from the marble floor. She knew a fall like she had could be bad news. She sighed before taking off down the hall, gingerly putting weight on the hip. She was relieved to see that she could move well with minimal pain. *I can feel my hips tightening up already, also a bump on my elbow and a pain in my foot. It won't do me any good to race through the halls. Lori will kill me for being late. This is happening just as I thought I was conquering my limp.*

Jade managed to barge through the door of the lecture room with less than two minutes to spare. Lori Meyers, her fellow student and best friend, stood inside the door waiting for her. "Where have you been? I was afraid you were going to be late. I see on the bulletin board out front that the new Head of Pediatrics has arrived to take over this class. I hear he is really great. They say he's tough maybe, but great. Let's get seated."

Jade saw a waste basket sitting inside the classroom door. She gave the broken clipboard a toss as she walked by. They looked for two places together. "This is like church. All the back seats are taken. We'll have to go to the second row to be together," Jade whispered as they searched the chairs.

"There are two seats together in the second row. We'd better take them," Lori whispered back.

Jade let out a sigh of relief as she plopped in a seat in the middle of the second row, directly in front of the speaker's stand. She started shifting her papers around to take notes when she saw one page of the stranger's notes. She groaned, "Oh, no, Lori. I have some guy's notes mixed in with mine. Oh well, his loss, I don't have the slightest idea who he was."

The Dean of nursing stepped up on the dais to introduce the lecturer. The short bald Dean droned, "It is with great pleasure that I can tell you that our new Head of Pediatrics has arrived just in time to present the first lecture for his class in Medical Ethics."

Jade felt a tingle of excitement. She had been waiting to take the Medical Ethics class from the first day she had decided to change her major to nursing. Almost a year after the accident that had left her with a badly injured left arm and hip, she had given up on playing the piano for any length of time. Even the shorter classical pieces left her wrist aching and her spirit exhausted. Both had been broken in the accident—the accident that had taken Ted's life, put her in the hospital for two and a half months, and left two-year-old Tommy in a coma. She barely remembered begging the doctors to save her little boy any way possible and nothing about the accident itself. Even after many months, she had no recollection of the accident itself. Bits and pieces of memory came to her at odd times.

She wondered more than once if she could have done something to prevent it happening. What had actually happened that day? Why would Ted pull into the path of a semi? By the time she awoke from her emergency surgeries, Tommy had lapsed into the coma that had held him away from her for over two years.

That first year, during her recovery and Tommy's illness, she had struggled to realign her life as a widow, the mother of a seriously ill child, and a soul adrift in indecision. The question of her own responsibility haunted her constantly. She intended to write her thesis for the Medical Ethics class about medical decisions made under duress. She was never quite sure if she would have told them to save Tommy if she had been lucid enough to realize just how serious his injuries had been. As a part of that, she intended to experiment with music as a method of bringing a comatose patient back to the real world. Tommy had always quieted and listened when she practiced the piano before the accident. She intended to play music for her little patients in whatever genre the parents preferred.

The Dean droned on, "I am pleased to present to you Dr. Jeffrey Davidson, our new Head of Pediatrics." Jade nearly fainted. There on the stage in front of her stood the stranger from the hall. The note page she held in her hand was part of his lecture notes. She slid down in her seat, hoping against hope that he wouldn't recognize her.

Jeff had entered the auditorium in a snit. He had nearly been late after taking a wrong hallway through the two-block-long hospital complex, ran into some bumbling woman, scattered his notes all over the floor, and now he found he was missing a page of his notes. He knew he would have to wing it for this lecture and use precious time rearranging all of his notes before the next lecture. Each point in his lectures was important for student nurses to learn. If he forgot one thing, it could be crucial for their future careers.

If not for that stupid woman, I would have been on time with my notes intact. Now I have to find time to redo my notes when I have a million things to do. Prepare notes, get acquainted with the layout of the hospital, tour the campus, find a house to buy, and prepare for complicated surgeries. But dang, she had beautiful eyes. What am I thinking? I don't have time to think about a woman. He was not in a good mood as he began to survey the crowded room before him. There were thirty-two nursing students signed up for the ethics class. He knew that alone would take up all of his spare time and that of the assistant they had assigned him.

As he surveyed the room, he suddenly caught a glimpse of long dark hair half covering a pretty face. Be darned if it didn't look like the woman from the hallway. Her head was down while she examined her notes so he couldn't be sure it was her. The blonde directly behind her was giving him flirtatious looks. He was mildly irritated. The last thing he needed was a student nurse going gaga over him. He placed his papers on the dais and began the lecture. The dark-headed woman in the second row continued to keep her head ducked so he couldn't see her face or her eyes clearly. In a moment, he was lost in the presentation, checking his notes as he turned the pages.

Jade listened to his deep voice as he talked. She loved his voice. There was something about it that turned her on. *What the hell? No one falls in love with a man because of his voice, do they? Stop it, Jade. Concentrate on the content of the lecture, not the contents of those great jeans.* She felt herself blushing.

Embarrassed by her own thoughts, she kept her head down to keep him from recognizing her as she took copious notes on the lecture. She was full of excitement over the content of the course. She knew she was going to love the class. She hoped that he wouldn't hold their first meeting against her. It would be too much to ask that he didn't recognize what a klutz she was because of the broken hip. Twenty minutes into the lecture, she was surprised when he stopped talking and began to shuffle through his lecture notes. After the second time, he searched through them, he announced, "I do apologize. I seem to have lost a page of my notes. I will have to recreate them for the next lecture. Leave a blank space in your notes, and I will fill it in next time." Jade wondered if she could find a hole to crawl into as he suddenly caught her eye.

With a weak smile, she waved the page of notes before him. The girl in front of her saw him staring at Jade and turned around, took the notes, and handed them to Jeff. "Well, well, well, my notes have suddenly appeared. It seems a hurried little nurse has found them for me. You may continue with your notes." The entire auditorium full of students laughed as he drew attention to Jade's flaming face before he returned to his lecture. He felt a pang of conscious when he noted tears pooling in the loveliest blue eyes he had ever seen. *Come on, Jeff. You don't have to be mean about it. She didn't run into you intentionally. Just because you are rushed getting into the swing of this job doesn't mean you should take it out on a student nurse.*

When the hour was over, Jade and Lori gathered their things to leave the room. "Jade, how did you get his notes?" Lori asked.

"Well, I literally fell for him. I'll tell you when we get home tonight," she told Lori as they walked along toward the elevators to Fifth floor. "I think I had better keep out of his way. They say he is really tough on students. I just hope he doesn't hold grudges."

Horror of horrors for Jade, Jeff Davidson stood just outside the lecture room door talking to the Dean and several students. There was no way she could get to the elevators without brushing past him. The blonde student, Penny Hansen, a fourth-year student, was trying to gain and monopolize Jeff's attention.

He listened with half an ear as Penny gushed over his lecture. "Oh, Dr. Davidson, that was wonderful. I am going to love this class. I already have an idea for my paper. I'll check with you in your office tomorrow to see if you like it."

He wished she would shut up. He had seen a dozen like her in the last three years of teaching ethics. He really would like to apologize to the dark-haired girl, but she was leaving the lecture room. A tingle went through him as she brushed against him as she left the room. He caught a whiff of some flowery perfume. He wondered what had just happened to him. He couldn't remember having those feelings with any other woman he had come into contact with since he was a freshman in high school and just noticing girls.

When he finally extracted himself from Penny and two other students with legitimate questions, the girl and her friend had disappeared down the hall. He assumed that he would be seeing her again soon if she were a student. He thought she might be a little older than the average student, but that wasn't unusual. He caught himself hoping he would see her soon, a most unusual reaction for him.

Back at the nurse's station on Fifth floor, Jade and Lori joined Maggie Hill and Lisa Kline, the nurses on duty for the unit. "How was the lecture? I heard that the new Head of Pediatrics was here a day early to start his duties. What was he like?" Maggie asked.

"The lecture was great," Lori told them. "I'm excited about the class."

"I thought he was a good lecturer, but I think he's a pompous ass," Jade told her as she picked up Tommy's chart and began to read through it as she walked toward his room.

"Wow, what brought that on?" Maggie asked. "Jade is usually so nice about people. She even says good things about Penny Hansen."

"I haven't had time to find out yet," Lori told her. "She said she literally fell for him. She'll tell me when we get back to our apartment." The nurses got busy as their little charges began to wake up. None of them had time to wonder about the new Head of Pediatrics.

Chapter 5

By the time Jeff returned from visiting after class with the Dean about rules and regulations, over three hours had passed, and he was hungry. He didn't like being in a new facility very well. He would have to ask someone how to find the cafeteria. The Dean had told him they would give him a full-scale tour at one thirty. He'd have to hurry to eat. Jeff stopped at the nurse's station on Fifth floor. "Excuse me," he said to Maggie. "Can you give me directions to the cafeteria?"

"Sure. You go down that hall to the left and take elevator C down to the basement. The cafeteria is on your right," Maggie told him.

"Thank you," he told her as he turned for the elevators.

Lori watched him go. She turned to Maggie. "Wow, there goes one good looking man. He was polite enough then. I wonder why Jade is so down on him already?"

At one thirty-five, the Dean arrived and led Jeff down the hallway to patient rooms. They examined each child as they went along. There were three with serious broken bones and four more with congenital handicaps that had been surgically repaired. The other eight little patients had various problems needing special care. As a teaching hospital, they received the worst cases in the state, either for treatment or as welfare patients.

They approached room 512. "This is our most baffling case," the Dean explained. "Tommy Barnes was brought in following head trauma in a car accident nearly three years ago. He's still comatose. We follow him daily, and he is hooked up to a feeding tube. We take scans on a regular basis. So far, there is no reason for him not to come around. He just doesn't respond to us."

Jeff took his time examining the child and made a cursory glance at the first two pages of the chart before commenting to the Dean, "He's in remarkably good condition for the extent of his injuries. Are you sure there are no signs of recovery?"

The Dean looked a bit uncomfortable. "Our last Head of Pediatrics, Dr. Porter, didn't have much interest in him. We considered that attitude of hopelessness when we agreed to let him retire early. He felt that ethically the child should have been allowed to die in the ER. The mother begged to save him. It seems her husband had just been killed in that same accident, and she was severely injured."

"I see a CD player over here on the table. I saw players in three other rooms too. What's going on with those?"

"I don't know. You'd have to ask one of the nurses who they belong to."

Jeff went back to his office after the Dean gave him a complete tour of the two-block-long hospital complex. He sat thinking about the patients. He knew the ones with broken bones were healing nicely and the ones following surgeries to correct their physical problems would improve. His greatest concern was the little comatose boy in 512. Where was he? Could he realize what was happening around him? Why hadn't his mind returned to his family? There were no ready answers to his questions. Jeff vowed to keep a close eye on the boy. It would be a challenge for him.

At their apartment that evening, Jade and Lori recounted the day as they sat eating popcorn and visiting in their pajamas and robes. Lori was surprised to hear about Jade's first meeting with the renowned Dr. Davidson. "I literally fell for him right there in the hallway when we collided. We dropped all of our papers together. We both sorted them, but that one page got mixed up in my work. He was really upset when he left me sitting there." She sighed. "He is one fine looking specimen of a man. All it would take is a Stetson hat to complete the picture of a perfect cowboy. I suppose that is the Oklahoma influence."

"Oh my gosh, Jade. I hope he doesn't hold that against you."

"So do I. I keep kicking myself for being such a klutz," Jade lamented.

"I can't believe you literally fell for him. He is a mighty good-looking man. Why don't you set your cap for him?"

"I don't need another man in my life, ever. Besides, I value my nursing career far too much to risk it making eyes at a faculty member." She laughed. "Remember, it is an ethics class."

Two days later, Jeff found Jade in Tommy's room when he went to observe the child during his spare time. She was checking Tommy's vitals and adjusting the bed sheets.

He watched her perform the routine duties before asking, "What is your prognosis on this child?"

Jade bristled. *Careful, he has a legitimate question. What do I realistically believe will happen with Tommy? As his mother, I kept holding out hope that he will return and be the bright little boy he was before the accident. As a nursing student, I have to look at it differently. I can't let my own feelings get in the way of my objectivity, especially when I answer Dr. Davidson.*

"I'm not sure, Doctor. As you know, it isn't my place to give a diagnosis."

Careful Jade, he may be trying to trip you up by making you do something outside your realm of responsibilities. She continued, "You realize, I'm just a student nurse. I will tell you that I keep that CD player in here as a part of my research into the effects of music on pediatric patients and their recovery. I ask the parents what type of music they usually listen to at home and play it for the child while they're here. If nothing else, I have noted that most of them will relax and go to sleep much easier." She winced. "I've even played Hard Rock for a couple, but they seem to respond well to it if it's what they're used to. I have to admit that I hope to reach Tommy through the music. It does seem to quiet him if he's restless."

"So you're the one who has placed the CDs in every room. I'll be interested to hear more about your thesis. That sounds like a worthy subject. Have you been keeping track of your data?"

"Yes, I have two years' worth now. I saved the data because I knew I wanted to write about music and children's recovery pace." She didn't mention that this Pediatric rotation was the first time she had included other children in her research. All of the rest of the time it had been Tommy and the CDs of her playing classical piano. Tommy had always reacted positively to her music from day one. He would calm down and go to sleep quickly. She could remember the nights when the colic was the worst, he would finally calm down when she resorted to playing music for him. She hoped that playing her music in the hospital would register somewhere in his brain. When she first got the idea, it was the only thing she could do to help her little boy. She still had no concrete evidence from Tommy to prove that it helped to play familiar music. The project had become her passion.

"I'll be supervising your thesis," Jeff told her. "Be sure to keep me up to date on your research, and don't miss the Thanksgiving deadline for your first draft."

"I won't, Doctor."

"Oh, by the way, how often do the parents visit this child?"

She was a little surprised by the question. "The mother comes at odd hours as often as possible. The father is dead. He died in the same wreck that injured Tommy. That information should be in the chart on page 3."

"I happen to think family members, especially mothers, are the most important visitors a kid can have. I hope Tommy's mother hasn't given up on visiting him."

Given up on Tommy? I've never given up on him. I sat by this bedside with casts on my arm and my hip in a stabilizer for hours at a time for the first three months he was here.

Every spare minute between therapy sessions for myself, I spent with Tommy, reading to him, talking to him, or playing music to him. I sat in that chair and prayed until I didn't know what to pray anymore. I cried over him, and I begged God to bring him back to me. I paid his bills and struggled with him through it all. I went back to my maiden name because I didn't want to be associated with the Barneses another minute. If Tommy were able to go to school, I might regret doing that, but right now, I don't. I don't know how much more this doctor can expect me to do. If I could just remember the details of the accident, I would feel more comfortable about the whole thing. She picked up her things and left the room.

Jeff noticed Jade in Tommy's room three mornings before the time for the students to check in. She was always playing her music or sitting in the recliner in his room for an hour or so before she got up and checked in for duty. One morning he discussed his concern with Maggie, "I see Jade Kennedy spends a lot of time in the Barnes boy's room. I'm not sure that's a good thing. There is a danger in getting too attached to one patient. I've never seen the mother here. Do you think Miss Kennedy is getting a little too involved with her patient?"

Maggie was astounded. "I don't see how you can think that. She does come in early to spend time with Tommy, but I think she does that only because of her thesis. I think it will be a great one."

"What little I know about it without looking at her outline, I think it sounds interesting. Just so she doesn't get too involved with one patient." He asked himself why he cared how much time she spent on her thesis. Maybe, just maybe, it was because he was drawn to the sadness in her eyes, a sadness he couldn't read or explain. No one person her age, twenty-five, he had seen on her records should carry that much sadness around with them. He wasn't sure why it mattered to him one way or the other. For the first time in his life, he seriously considered a woman he wanted in his life.

Chapter 6

When Maggie asked if he was going to the department's annual fall picnic the next weekend, he wondered if it might give him a chance to meet with others in the hospital. The picnic was held on a mild autumn day. Jeff had been happy to hear it would be a catered affair. He arrived at the Riverside Park at eleven thirty. Over fifty members of the hospital staff attended the event. For the first time, Jeff spotted Jade in tight-fitting jeans. They looked every bit as good as he thought they would. She wore a red cotton top and had pulled her long hair back in a ponytail that made her look younger than her years. He didn't realize his heart was on his sleeve until Maggie walked up behind him and commented, "I see you are eying Jade. If you don't want everyone to know, you need to keep your heart to yourself."

He grinned sheepishly. "Oh, Maggie. I don't know how I'm going to do that, especially when she looks so great in those jeans. I have been thinking she looked good in scrubs, but I like her in those jeans even better."

"You had better sign up for the sack race as her partner. We'll be assigning partners randomly, but I can rig the pairs if you'd like." Her eyes twinkled. "I know it's a little underhanded, but I could manage to get it done for you."

"I'd like that Maggie, just so she won't back out if I'm her partner."

Jade was amazed when heard that Jeff was her partner. She recovered enough to laugh as they were handed a gunnysack. Jeff was pleased when Jade got into the spirit of the game. "Woohoo, Doctor, I want you to know that I'm a poor partner these days. I used to win all the sack races at home, but lately, I'm a little clumsy as you well know. You may have to carry me through this." She slipped her arm around his waist and held up the gunnysack Maggie handed her.

My God, her arm feels good around my waist. I wonder what it would feel like to hold her properly in my arms. He brought himself back to the moment. "Glad to oblige," Jeff told her as they struggled to step into the sack. Jade positioned herself on his right side.

"I think I can do better on this side," she told him. "You may have to catch me if my hip gives out. If we can get in sync, I should be able to keep up with you." They stood waiting for the starting whistle to announce the beginning of the race. *Boy, does she ever feel good in my arms. This sack has us tied close to each other. I will enjoy this race. I wonder what she's thinking.* They moved forward, tripping a time or two before they established a workable rhythm. Jade thought it took a little more time than necessary for Maggie to blow the whistle. She and Jeff took off. The first few steps were precarious. Jade began to laugh hysterically as they rushed along. Jeff thought he had never heard a more delightful sound. After hopping together for thirty yards, they stumbled across the finish line in second place.

They heard the announcement from the portable loud-speaker. Jade lay laughing at their dilemma. They lay in a pile at the finish line. Jeff wondered what it would be like if he lowered his head a bit and kissed that tempting mouth.

She broke the spell between them when she finally struggled to a sitting position and said, "Let me up. I think if I sit up, we can get out of this sack."

Without thinking, he told her, "I was enjoying the nearness."

She looked at him for a long time. *His eyes are so beautiful. They are as blue gray as the cloudy sky. I could find myself liking this doctor way too much.* He had no way of knowing that she was thinking, *I can't be falling for him.*

He's faculty, and there are rules against student relationships. If something happened between them, it would be her that would be dismissed; and as a doctor, he would probably get off with a reprimand. He missed his chance when she lowered her head and began to extricate herself from the gunnysack. They were so close he wanted to tip her head up a slight bit and kiss her delectable mouth. She gave him a long look before struggling to her feet as the sack fell away between them. He thought she turned a bit red with embarrassment. Without saying a word, she turned and walked away from him. The rest of the afternoon she avoided him. Jeff watched her laughing and talking with Maggie and the other partygoers. He felt a pang of jealousy when one of the interns hugged her as he left the park. He wondered why it bothered him so. She was just a student. He left, thinking what a fun day it had been.

A month after he arrived on campus, Jeff decided to take a walk away from the hospital. He walked through a beautiful residential area of older houses. Most were large, large enough for a big family. He noticed a "for sale" sign in one of the bigger yards. The property had a main house, a garage, and another, probably a servants' house, in the side yard of the acre-sized lot. He liked the looks of it, but it was rather large for one person. He would like the larger house, but he didn't know what he would do with the extra house. It wasn't particularly large. Maybe he would hire a student to keep up the yard, even a couple to do housework and yard work. He knew he wouldn't have to think about that until spring. The fall season was almost over, and all he would need would be snow removal.

The campus area around the hospital was hilly, and he was soon puffing a bit. He told himself he needed to find the gym facilities they had promised him with his contract. He wandered over campus, looking at the various buildings and enjoying the beauty of the numerous trees on campus. Giant maples grew around the Old Capitol Complex. He liked the various colors of those and rows of yellow ging-koes along the sidewalks. He vowed to attend at least one of the Hawkeye football games before the season was over. He passed the engineering department and the library before he crossed the Iowa River to return to the hospital com-plex. Off to his right he saw a newer glass-front building. The map he had of campus showed it to be the Performing Arts building.

As he turned to view the area, he saw Jade hurrying up the sidewalk toward the building. He was delighted to see her out of the hospital setting again. The delight-ful sound of her laughter echoed in his dreams at night. He determined to follow her. He really wanted to talk to her when they were both off duty. He knew there was a rule against student and professor liaisons, but he vowed he only wanted to know her a little better. She intrigued him, especially the sadness in her large blue eyes.

Jade seemed to be in a hurry. She entered the building ahead of him and disappeared inside. He followed into the strange place and looked around to see where she had gone. He went in a second set of doors and entered a hallway that branched off in both directions. She was nowhere in sight. He stood looking around when he heard her voice down the left hall. "Yes, I'm ready. You can put me down for that date. I can hardly wait."

An older, rather rotund, balding man followed Jade into the hall. Jade did not see Jeff standing there as she turned back toward the man. Jeff cringed when the older man pulled his wire-rimmed glasses down and looked at Jade. He heard him say, "I'm delighted to hear that you have accepted my invitation. It will be so nice to have you with me. I'll see you then." Jeff cringed when the man gave Jade a big hug.

I've seen enough. She's making a date with that man. What the hell? He must be thirty years older than she is. Come on, Davidson, he told himself. *Don't ever act like a jealous fool. You had to realize that someone a beautiful as Jade Kennedy would have a boyfriend, if you could call someone like that older man a boyfriend. You can't let it bother you.* But it did bother him. He couldn't say exactly why, but it bothered him a lot as he turned and hurried from the building, hoping she hadn't seen him there.

To take his mind off of what he had seen and heard in the Arts Building, Jeff had begun to search for a house. The small room in the Union was furnished by the university while he was looking for a house as a part of his contract, but it was like living in a motel. He wanted something with plenty of space and lots of light. He called a real estate agent he had heard one of the other doctor's mention.

They made an appointment to meet after she had found a list of houses for him to tour. Even though he was excited about looking for a house, Jeff found himself being short with the student nurses when they came for consultations on their papers. He knew he was being an ass but refused to admit to himself the cause. He snapped at Maggie and Lisa. When Penny Hansen slipped into his office and asked to talk about her "paper," he cut her short. She left in a huff, muttering, "He'll be sorry for treating me like that."

Maggie and Lisa discussed his surliness. "I don't know what's eating him," Lisa told Maggie. "I haven't changed procedures at all, and now he decides I'm doing it all wrong. I'd like to bonk him on the head and bring him back around."

Several days later, after catching Jeff watching Jade walk down the halls, Maggie speculated to Lisa, "I'm beginning to think I know what his problem is." She smiled to herself. "I really think I know. I'll tell you when I'm sure."

"I'm glad you've figured it out. I sure haven't," Lisa called over her shoulder as she headed for room 512 with Tommy's nourishment.

Maggie began watching Jeff and Jade. Within a week, she had determined that there was a strong attraction between them. Jeff looked forlorn whenever Jade disappeared down the hallways as she worked with the children. Jade would often stop what she was doing and watch Jeff as he hurried about the department. She hoped Jeff wouldn't push the relationship too much for it meant too much to Jade to finish the nursing program for her to risk it all on a fling with a faculty member. She thought it was sad, for they would make a stunning couple.

During the next shift, Jeff cornered Jade in Tommy's room. "I see that the chart says the previous director didn't hold out much hope for this kid to recover. How do you think he's doing?"

Jade hesitated a moment before commenting. He couldn't possibly know how many hours she had worried about the notes the director put in Tommy's chart. He couldn't possibly know how many tears she had shed when she read his negative comments. Carefully she answered, "I think this patient is more restless than usual. Sometimes I think he is trying to come out of it. Then he lays for hours without moving. It would take someone with much more training than I have to determine what is happening with him."

Jeff examined Tommy. "It could be a good sign if he is restless. I need to do some more research on what we can expect from him. It's a touchy thing to have a child this size in a coma. We can predict nothing about his future. If his derelict mother would show up once in a while, it might help decide if he will ever recover. Keep watch over him," he called back to her as he left the room.

Jade came out of Tommy's room fifteen minutes later, with tears in her eyes. "What's the matter?" Maggie asked.

"That…that Davidson. I could spit nails, I'm so mad."

"What did he do?"

"He made a really snide comment about Tommy's 'derelict mother. She never comes to see him,' he says," as she mimicked his comments. "How can a mother neglect him like that? He asks me that."

"Come on, Jade. Just tell him you're Tommy's mother," Maggie advised. "The most I will tell him is to take time to read the whole chart, page three included. It might open his blind eyes for him." She stood fuming. "And don't you tell him either. Let him find out any way he can."

She looked pleadingly at Maggie. "Promise you won't tell him."

Maggie grudgingly promised.

A group of Fifth-floor personnel attended an Iowa Hawkeye football game in early October. Jeff joined them on an overcast Saturday. He looked around for Jade but was disappointed when she didn't join the group. Maggie was there with her husband, Don Hill. The crowd was worked up for a game with Minnesota. Jeff was thankful he wasn't in the student section where he could see male students without shirts and painted torsos or face paints holding forbidden beer cans high over their heads. A card section held up cards that formed the Hawkeye logo. The noise from the standing students and the pep band filled the air. Jeff enjoyed the spectacle before him in spite of his wish that Jade had joined them. Three hours after the beginning kickoff, Iowa left the field, victorious over Minnesota. He gathered that was a great accomplishment for the teams were bitter rivals.

He had gotten enough nerve to ask Maggie, "Why didn't Miss Kennedy join us today? I didn't see that she had to work."

"You'll find out Jade hates football. She had a really bad experience her freshman year and hasn't attended a game here since. Then she doesn't particularly like big crowds either."

"What a shame. I thought she might be here today." Maggie smiled to herself. She was right. Jeff was falling for Jade. In spite of the fact that it would be inadvisable for them to pursue a relationship until Jade finished her program, Maggie hoped it would work out for them.

Jeff found himself observing Jade in class and in the halls of Fifth floor. He tried to open a conversation with her several times; but she merely answered his questions shortly, spoke politely, and moved quickly on. He considered ways to get her to stop and talk with him. Finally, he decided to approach Jade concerning her thesis. It was the best excuse he could think of to get her to talk with him.

The next time he met her in the hallway, he said, "I really would like to go over your thoughts with you before the outline is due. I do like your topic, and I would like to see evidence that you are doing the proper research. I want to double-check it before the deadline." *What are you doing, Davidson? You're making up a chance to spend time with her. Be careful, she's a student. She has a boyfriend who hugs her, and you are a staff member who knows better than to go after a student. Admit it, Davidson, you want to hug her.*

Jade finally agreed to meet with him concerning the thesis in late October. She appeared in his office with her notes in hand. He examined her research notes. "I'm impressed with your work. I see you have quite a number of cases. How did you get this many cases recorded?"

"I'm sure you are well aware that I have spent some time with Tommy Barnes. I was in ER my first rotation. I did a paper concerning children's injuries at that time. He was the main patient for that paper so I have an interest in his progress. By the way, have you any new ideas on his prognosis?"

"Not really. At least nothing I'm ready to disclose. I keep wondering if there is any pattern to his restless episodes, but I have to admit I am too busy to spend adequate time watching him. I really would like to see you spend less time with him. It appears to me that you're getting too involved with him. As a nurse, you need to learn to keep yourself distanced emotionally. It will help your mental attitude in the long run."

"I'm sure it would, but I couldn't be any more involved than I am, Doctor. I will admit that he is special to me."

"Control it, Miss Kennedy. It will wear you down if you let these patients get to you."

She jumped up, frustrated with his attitude. "There are a lot of things in this life that wear you down, Dr. Davidson. A sick little boy is only one of them." She hoped she hadn't said too much. She glanced at her watch to distract him. "I have to go. I have a class to get ready for," she said as she hurried out before she began to cry.

Damn him, if he would only read the whole chart. I shouldn't let him get to me like this. I can learn so much from him if the ethics class is any indication. I don't understand him. He baffles me as much as Ted did. She was shocked at that thought. *What is the matter with me? Am I still going to let Ted control my life? Why do I keep wondering if the accident was partly my fault? What really happened to cause that accident? What did I do?* She sighed. *I thought I was through this. I have to keep my distance from the good doctor until I figure all this out.*

Jade kept her word. She managed to avoid any close contact with Jeff. She hurried in and out of the ethics class. She nodded when she met him in the halls. She pretended to be deep in conversation with others if she saw him coming. She continued to visit Tommy on her off hours after checking to see if Jeff was in surgery or out of the building. She sat by Tommy's bedside holding his hand.

Occasionally she ran her thumb across his palm and kissed it. More than once she laid her head on his bed and cried for what might have been. She tried to keep herself from wondering, *What if... I can't keep asking myself what if. I have to stay strong. Now Professor Taylor is pushing me to plan my senior concert before Thanksgiving so I can get a double major when I graduate next semester. I told him I would do the concert, but I'm not sure I have the stamina. I'll have to spend hours practicing to get enough strength to play that long. Maybe one of the physical therapy girls can give me exercises to help build my wrist strength.*

She worked her left hand. Could she do it? Could she finish her nursing degree and also her Music degree? She knew it was a huge undertaking, but it should be worth it. She had accepted that her left arm and her left hip would never allow her the stamina she would need to play with the Symphony for hours on end, but if she could manage to pull off the concert, there would be a sense of total satisfaction that would boost her fragile self-confidence. She hoped to become a charge nurse that worked with paperwork enough to allow her to sit while she worked and baby the hip, at least for a while. She was quite sure the hip had improved. She no longer limped unless she was on her feet for too many hours or if she became extremely tired.

Jade spent every spare minute at the Music Building practicing for the concert scheduled for the Friday night before Thanksgiving. One afternoon, Jeff saw her leaving the building by the far north door. He walked after her but turned back when she headed for the Performing Arts Center. He wondered why he felt so down. She had the right to meet with and date anyone she wished. If she could date a music professor, why couldn't she date him? She seemed to be so set against it.

Chapter 7

Tommy spiked a fever late one evening just before she was to leave for the day. She steeled herself to the fact that he might have picked up a serious infection. Ignoring Jeff's warnings to stay away from Tommy, she spent the night in the recliner next to his bed, watching every move he made. Once or twice, she wondered if he was fighting to awaken or if it was only the fever bothering him.

She slept only a short time in the recliner with her feet propped up. She watched Tommy as the fever raged. It was very late when his fever broke, and he quieted once more. Relieved that he seemed to be better, she fell asleep in the chair. She awoke when Jeff entered the room on his early rounds. He was shaking her by the shoulder. "Miss Kennedy, What are you doing here?" he asked gruffly.

She brushed her hair out of her eyes as she blinked herself awake. He noted that she looked beautiful even though she had just woken up. She struggled up in the chair. "Tommy had a high fever last night, and I decided that I needed to stay with him."

"So you decided to take the place of his neglectful mother and stay with him yourself. I would like to give you this suggestion as an order. Distance yourself from this child."

She stared at him incredulously. *I stayed with him like any other mother would have done.* Anger filled her. No matter what the consequences were, she could not keep from saying, "Dr. Davidson, I stayed on my own time. I don't think you have the authority to keep me out of this room on my own time. I will arrange to keep out of Tommy's room during my working shifts if that will make you happy. You can be assured that I will be asking to have one of the other instructors take over my thesis. I can only hope you will not be vindictive enough to flunk me in the course. I will do my best to live up to your standards in class time only." She stalked out of the room before she burst into tears. Maggie watched her enter the women's bathroom and slam the door behind her. Jeff stomped out of Tommy's room behind her and walked by the nurses' station to his office.

Jade cried in the bathroom. Jeff paced in his office. His temper did not improve as he contemplated his latest encounter with Jade. "What in the world is the matter with you, Dr. Davidson?" he asked himself sarcastically. "All you do is antagonize Jade. She looked like you had slapped her when you ordered her to distance herself from Tommy Barnes. What does she think she's doing? What is she trying to accomplish by spending so much time with that one kid? Why does it bother me so much? It irks me that she's right. I don't have any authority to tell her how to spend her free time." He sat down in his chair and held his head in his hands. "Why does this bother me so much? Can I be falling for a woman who wants nothing to do with me? I've never had a problem getting a woman to like me until now. What am I doing wrong? I have never wanted to let a woman interfere in my career. Jade gets to me though." He jumped up again. *Oh, my God. I can't be falling in love with her.* He threw a pen on his desk and stomped out to the nurses' desk, asked for several charts to read before he made his morning rounds, and returned to his office to read.

Maggie watched him enter his office. "I'm right. He is falling for Jade. Poor dumb bastard, he's really lost it over Jade. I want to tell him she's Tommy's mother so bad, but I know Jade would never forgive me if I do. Maybe I can figure out some way to make her realize he's falling for her. I would like to see her find someone who would take care of her for a change."

Jeff came out of his office to make rounds thirty minutes later. Maggie and Lisa followed him, taking notes as they moved from room to room. At Tommy's bedside, the women watched Jeff examine the little boy. "Do you see anything for our report?" Maggie asked.

Jeff stood and watched Tommy for a long time. "Has this child responded to anyone?"

"Not that we are aware of, sir. If he does, it has never been observed, or it would be in the chart. It does say he gets very restless at times," Lisa answered him.

"Are you seeing something?" Maggie asked hopefully.

"I'm not sure. There's nothing I can put my finger on. I've been reading up on what to expect from a comatose patient. The restlessness is a pretty normal sign. I'd like to see him open his eyes or even talk a bit. I understand that would be something we could hope for. It wouldn't mean he was out of the coma, but it would be a sign of improvement." Jeff stood observing Tommy for another minute.

"I guess I just have a feeling there is something happening with him that I can't see."

"It would certainly be a relief to his mother if he would improve," Lori told.

"Where the hell does that woman live anyway? I have other mothers who manage to make it here from the western part of the state on a regular basis. I've never caught his mother here. If she didn't come see him before too long, we just won't know if he remembers her or not."

Maggie persisted, "But, Doctor, I think she is here more than you realize."

"What do you mean? I've never seen her." Maggie raised an eyebrow at Lisa.

Lisa commented, "It should be in the chart on page three about his family. I understand the father is dead. I've heard that might be a blessing. I'm sure it will tell you all about the mom."

"I don't have time to read anymore charts than I do. The medical facts are all I need."

Maggie shrugged, and Lisa rolled her eyes. The three completed rounds. On a hunch, Jeff walked back to Tommy's room and stood watching the still form.

Tommy was a beautiful golden-haired child. He had been sick so long that he was very small for his age. Jeff wondered what color his eyes were behind the closed eyelids. Gently he opened an eyelid. The eyes were blue. They reminded him of the color of someone else's eyes, but he couldn't put his finger on who it was.

Suddenly, Jeff thought he saw a slight eye movement. So slight that he wasn't sure it had actually happened. He watched for fifteen more minutes but saw no additional signs of eye movement behind the closed eyelids. He walked slowly back to his office, considering what new procedures might be available to help the child. He had read that there were some new physical therapy procedures that seemed to help comatose patients retain their physical strength. He stopped at the nurses' desk and wrote an order for some daily physical therapy. He gave specific routines he wanted tried, for they would be in addition to the routine exercises required for every patient. He went to his office, trying to figure out exactly what was bothering him about Tommy's case. If he could just put his finger on it, he could, yes, he could answer a lot of questions.

Chapter 8

Maggie greeted Jeff the next morning as he came out of Tommy's room. "Are you done with rounds?" she asked.

"No, I was just watching Tommy. I'm not sure, but I have a feeling things are happening with him. I wish I knew what was going on in that little head of his."

"I think we all would. Sometimes we pray for miracles. We don't always get the answer we want. Sometimes the answer is no."

Later that day, he happened to see Jade entering Tommy's room after she was off for the day. He followed her into the room. "I see you have decided not to take my advice to stay away from this child."

"Doctor, I told you I am on my own time. I don't intend to stop spending time here."

"If I ever catch his mother here, I'll give her a piece of my mind," he told her as he turned and left the room.

Jade went back to the desk several minutes later, trying to control her emotions. Maggie walked up to her. "I can see by your face that things didn't go well in there," she said to Jade.

"No, they didn't. I get so mad at him I could cry or scream or shoot him."

Maggie tried to get her to laugh. "Don't make threats like that. I don't want to have to appear in court in your defense."

Jade picked up materials to take home for the evening. "See you tomorrow," she called as she left for the apartment. She fumed as she walked past Jeff's office door. "I'd like to teach him a valuable lesson or two. He certainly needs some sensitivity training."

An hour later, Maggie looked up to see Jeff coming down the hallway. "Are you still around? It's past time for all good little doctors to go home for some rest."

"I'm on my way, I think. It seems like I never have much free time. I've never figured out your schedule, Maggie. It seems you are always here. Lisa too."

"Oh, most of us have a little time off. I'm only here now because I forgot my keys again. I can't seem to break the habit of losing them. I don't work this weekend."

They looked up to see Jade coming up the hall with a sack from the cafeteria in her hand.

"Suppertime?" Maggie asked her.

"Yes, I'm going to eat in Tommy's room before I go home for the night," she told Maggie as she walked down the hall, ignoring Jeff.

"Does she ever have any time off?" Jeff asked Maggie.

"Jade? I'm sure she does, but she's pretty busy. With her classes, her thesis, and her—"

He interrupted, "I'd like to schedule another research meeting with her. She doesn't even have time for a short coffee break to discuss it."

Maggie hesitated before answering. "Are you talking about Jade? I think she's pretty busy right now. I'm sure things will slow down for her after the Thanksgiving break. By the way, what are you doing for Thanksgiving, Doctor?"

"I don't have anything planned. My family is so scattered we only try for Christmas and the fourth of July to get together. One year, Mom even had Christmas on the fourth of July when none of us could get home in December."

"Wow, that sounds a little hectic. I'm pretty sure that's where Jade is right now. There's a lot of things going on in her life this semester. Give her a little time. She'll work it in."

"She probably won't if I'm involved."

Maggie raised her left eyebrow. "Oh?"

He leaned on the counter and confided. "Haven't you noticed that she avoids me like the plague? I'd like to get to know her a little better, learn more about her research and all that, but she keeps me at arm's length. You'd think I had bad breath or body odor."

Maggie laughed. "I'm sure that's not the problem. That Obsession you wear drives us all nuts. Only a rich man or one with very good taste can afford that."

"Well, the smell of money must not attract her."

Jade suddenly walked up behind him. "Money doesn't attract who?"

He flushed. "Just a woman I know. How about you, Miss Kennedy? Does money attract you?"

"I haven't a clue. I haven't seen enough of it lately to know." *There was nothing left over after I paid off the bills for Ted's funeral each month, my rehab and Tommy's care. Thank heaven we had good insurance that I have been able to keep*

72

as long as I pay the premium. No matter how long I wear my clothes or how little I eat, there isn't much left over after I keep up on that premium. If only Ted's parents had seen their way clear to help me with some of the funeral and medical expenses, I wouldn't have had to put Tommy on Medicaid. Turning to Maggie, she divulged, "I do know having student loans and a lot of debts will attract my money before I get a chance to decide what I'd like to do with it. Maybe when I'm done with school, I can think of vacations and holidays. Right now, those are out of the question until I'm through nurse's training and probably for fifteen years after that."

He turned to her and asked, "What does attract you, Ms. Kennedy?"

Without taking time to think who she was talking to, she rattled off, "Music, especially classical, good food, the theater, historical novels, hiking, as if I ever get to do that anymore, lying in the cancer-inducing sun, antique hunting, museums and historic sights, the Rocky Mountains, Civil War stories, especially *Gone with the Wind*, and kids. How about you, Doctor?"

"Well, the hiking and the classical music and the theater are good for me, as well as the food and museums. The rest are just memories from times before medical school. Most of the kids I see would just as soon start screaming when they see me come in their rooms."

"I know you are a Pediatric surgeon and don't have much time away from the hospital. What about the kids? Do you like them as little people or just as a medical challenge? Do you approach them as scared little people or only a surgical case?"

He thought a while before answering, "I like kids. It's just that most of them that I see are here as medical challenges. I suspect they are not at their best during such trying circumstances. I guess I never thought about how they want to be treated. It must be pretty scary for them to be here."

"I know they are scared. You have to take extra time and connect with them before they start seeing you as a person, not a doctor who hurt them."

He was a bit uncomfortable with the conversation. Deep down, he felt she might be right. To change the subject, he said, "Look, Jade. I really would like to meet with you about your research. Isn't there a time you can see me for about an hour?"

"I've already told you, Dr. Davidson, after Thanksgiving. If you don't plan to leave town for the holiday, why don't we meet the day after Thanksgiving? I'll be done with my big project by then, and I'll have plenty of time that day. It's one of the few we students have off."

Maggie broke in. "I have an idea. Why don't the two of you come to my house for Thanksgiving dinner? Our kids aren't coming until Sunday, and I happen to have the day off. I love to cook for someone besides myself and Don. I always ask a nurse and the few interns who can't get home either. Of course, I would insist that you bring a salad or a dessert."

"Sounds great to me," Jade accepted. "I'll bring pumpkin pie and whipped cream."

Jeff laughed. "Guess that leaves me with a caterer's salad. I assume one of those cranberry things is in order. Hy-Vee makes them all the time."

"Perfect," Maggie replied. "I'll give you the time and address later. Now I have to get to work."

"Me too," Jade echoed as she turned and hurried down the hall.

And me three, Jeff thought as the two women turned away from him and went about their respective duties. The thought of Thanksgiving with Jade under "normal" circumstances appealed to him. He wondered why she wasn't spending time with her man friend, unless he was married. For some reason, that thought brought him comfort. If the guy was married, he couldn't offer Jade much. That old guy was probably just leading her on to dump her when it wasn't convenient for him.

He walked away, whistling softly at that he would be able to see her out of her nursing student behavior and away from the hospital setting. He wondered if she wore those great jeans outside the hospital. The nice tight ones she had worn to the picnic. Humming to himself, he went to his office.

The second week of November. An early season snow storm blew into the state. It turned bitter cold as small flakes blew through the air, obscuring visibility for drivers on Interstate 80. Small drifts piled up around the city. Everyone wore snow boots and heavy clothing. Jade arrived at the hospital for classes on Monday morning with glints of water drops in her hair from melting snow flakes. She met Jeff coming down the hallway. They greeted each other and moved on. *Oh my, she is beautiful*, Jeff thought as he walked toward surgery.

Jade, Maggie, and Lori hurried down a glassed hallway together on their way to Fifth floor. They could see the snow swirling about the outdoor garden. Lori carried on about the weather. "This stuff is so beautiful—from inside. It's really nasty today. The wind is terrible, and the snow is so wet and heavy it almost suffocates you. I know this is Iowa, and it always changes. I wish it wouldn't change so quickly though. I hope we can get home tonight."

Maggie and Jade agreed with her. "If we can't, we'll probably have the chance to take over double shifts to cover for those who can't get in. It'll be a good chance for us to pick up some overtime hours. They don't talk like it'll be over until late tomorrow afternoon."

"You're right. It'll probably be double shift for us. Most of the student nurses can come across from the dorm through the tunnel. It'll be the ones who live away from the hospital area that'll have the most trouble getting here." They chatted as they entered the nurses' lounge and took off boots and coats and put them in the closet. "Want to make a bet as to when it will stop?" Lori asked.

"No way. I can't. I might lose and have to take out a loan to pay you," Jade groaned. "Wonder if everyone will make it to class?"

"Probably. We seldom get a break from class."

From behind them, a deep voice asked, "Do you need one?" *Damn*, Jade thought as she jumped from surprise. *What is wrong with me? Why does his presence make me so jumpy? I love to hear his voice during lectures. I'd recognize that voice anywhere. I can't be falling for him*, she told herself. *I just can't.*

Lori looked around. Jeff was standing behind her. "Not really, Dr. Davidson. It's just student nature to think they've really accomplished something great if they don't have a class once in a while."

He poured himself a cup of coffee and leaned against the edge of the counter. "I remember those days. Worst thing was I never heard the news in time to be able to snuggle back in bed and sleep. I was always up, dressed and in the classroom before the announcement was made. When I reached that point, I kept on working at something. There was always something to do."

"That's where I am now," Jade moaned. "There's always something to do. I'm just pleased that I seem to be holding up well enough physically to get it all done." She checked her hair in the mirror and left the room. Jeff watched her appreciatively.

"Why would a young woman like her be concerned about holding up physically, Lori? I thought I saw her limping several times. Does she have a physical problem?"

"Yes, sir. I thought everyone knew all about her." *It's about time he found out a little bit about Jade.* "Her left side was badly injured in a car accident a couple of years ago," she told him. *Jade will kill me if she knows I've told him that much, but I think he should know about her.* "It's almost completely healed now. I only notice the limp if she's overly tired."

"She does pretty well if that's the problem."

"Jade does very well at whatever she tries. I really admire her. Most of us around here do." Her silence indicated that he didn't. "I'd better get busy too. I'm subbing here today. It keeps me hopping."

He watched her head for the door. "Have a good day."

She started, "Well, thanks, Doctor. I'll try."

Chapter 9

The storm continued throughout the afternoon and into the evening hours. As predicted, nurses all over the area called in to say they couldn't get out of their driveways and public transportation was limited to a few blocks of the campus center routes. Jade and Lori both agreed to take over extra shift duties for those who couldn't get to work. At 1:00 a.m., a 911 call came in to emergency. The dispatcher called Pediatrics. "There are two children arriving in fifteen minutes."

According to the paramedics, there are broken bones and some cuts and bruises. "They're coming in ambulances with a snowplow in front of them. It happened out on I-80 right here in the city limits. We are hoping it isn't too serious. We're really shorthanded down here tonight."

"We'll meet them at emergency," Jeff informed the dispatcher. "Be there in ten." Jeff hung up the phone. He stood with a frown on his face, thinking over the possibilities. With two injured children, he would need plenty of help. He looked around the floor to see how many were on duty. "Do you have any help here, Jade?"

She raised an eyebrow. What was he wanting from her? "Yes, Ellie made it in about twelve thirty. She walked more than three blocks through the storm to get here after her car got stuck. She says it's terrible out there. She was very late, but at least she's here. Penny usually works with her, but she called in that she couldn't make it across town from her apartment."

"I'm going to need help in emergency and ER. There aren't enough nurses to go around. Would you consider going down to ER with me? I'll see to it you get overtime pay for helping me. The most you will have to do is obey my orders."

"Of course, I'll help. I can use extra money any time. Lisa can do this floor alone until we get the two new ones up here anyway. You might be interested to know I served in the emergency clinical my first rotation, so I do have some experience with injured kids and the layout of the ER department."

"Great, I'll get my own emergency kit and be right with you." He came back out of his office a couple of minutes later carrying a small bag.

As they walked down the long hallways, Jade found the silence between them beginning to bother her. She started to talk a little nervously. "Lisa said it's terrible out there. I can't believe it's storming like this so early in November. There's over eight inches of snow in places and the wind is creating white-out conditions on the highways. I've been in that a couple of times. It's frightening to say the least."

"I've never been out in one of these storms, but I understand they're tricky. We got mostly ice storms in Oklahoma." He asked her, "Was it storming when your wreck happened?"

She looked at him incredulously as details she had struggled two years to remember flashed back to her. Ted had been screaming at her, at other drivers, and Tommy when he began crying. Ted had received word the day before that his work performance was in need of improvement, and he wasn't taking it well. As far as he was concerned, no one had the right to question his actions. She had only half listened as he raged on about his boss, her own lack of interest in his interests, her sissy musical career, and the screaming brat in the back seat. Jade closed her eyes and swayed a bit. It was the first time she had remembered those details about the wreck other than those in her dreams. She saw clearly Ted reaching toward the back seat to hit at Tommy's legs as he yelled, "Stop screaming before I stop and beat the shit out of you." He turned to her and yelled, "If you hadn't—" It had been that moment of distraction that had caused Ted to career into the path of the truck. It had been the comment that had haunted Jade since the accident. It was the one she recalled over and over, "If you hadn't—"

She had wondered many times if Ted's comment had made her believe it was somehow her fault. *If I hadn't what?* What had Ted been trying to say to her? All she remembered was the blackness and the noise. Ted screamed in agony, and Tommy lay still between them. The pain overwhelmed her, and she passed out.

There had been a blank where hours of important things had taken place. Jade had learned later that Ted had not bothered to secure the car seat properly, allowing Tommy, car seat and all, to slam over the front seat and into the dashboard. It had all been Ted's fault. The realization that it was not her fault hit her hard. She turned deathly pale and swiped her hand across her brow.

Jeff grabbed at her to steady her. "Are you all right, Miss Kennedy? I'm so sorry. I had no business asking that. It's just that I heard you had been injured in a wreck a couple of years ago."

She gained her composure. "No, it's all right. It was actually almost three years ago, and it was perfect summer weather," she answered flatly. "I had never recalled a lot of the details of the accident until this moment. My husband was having a fit of rage. He wasn't watching where he was going. I didn't remember that exact detail until right now. Now I remember why the accident happened. Now I remember that it wasn't my fault. Now I remember why I hate him so." She swiped a lock of hair away from her face. "I'm sorry. I lost it for a moment there."

He wanted to take her in his arms and offer comfort, but he knew it was not the thing to do. He merely advised her, "Come on, Jade. Take a deep breath. Everyone can lose control. Have you been able to forgive him?"

He had just called her Jade. *I hope he isn't getting too familiar.* She looked him in the eye and asked flatly, "How do you forgive a dead man, Doctor? He died shortly after the crash in the ER. I could hear him dying from the room I was in. They were pushing me to make decisions. I was seriously hurt too. I remember feeling absolutely nothing when they told me Ted was dead. There were times I wish I had died too."

"Surely not."

Oh yes, I did, when they told me Tommy was in a coma and when I spent weeks struggling to walk again. Most of all, I wanted to die as I made funeral arrangements from a hospital bed. "When I," she answered, "only in the beginning. Everything I had planned to do with my life changed in that moment." *All the dreams and plans I had for my son died with the accident.* "As I healed, nursing began to appeal to me. I admired the nurses who cared for me and other patients." *A lot of things changed, my music included, but he doesn't need to know any of that.* "I got interested in the research and the nursing program. Some other parts of my life began to gel once again. I never feel that way now. I'm so glad you asked the question. Now I remember so much more about the wreck."

He was grateful that she had told him a bit about her life. Maybe if they worked well together this day, he might be able to start over with her. "Good. Now we'd better hurry. I think I hear the ambulances coming."

Chapter 10

The next three hours passed in a blur as the two of them stood side by side, desperately working to comfort and care for the two badly injured children. Jeff was impressed by Jade's ability to calm them even in the worst moments of the initial examinations. It wasn't easy to examine a screaming, fighting child who was already scared by all of the strange surroundings and their own pain. They resorted to a sheet wrap on the seven-year-old boy when he tried to fight them. In order to prevent him from further injuring himself, they literally rolled him in the sheet until he could not fight them anymore.

When he finally calmed enough for Jeff to question him, he sobbed out the story. "Daddy couldn't see. Something hit us real hard in the back of the car." He whined miserably. "Where's my mom and dad? I want my mom and dad."

"They'll be coming soon. What's your name, son?"

"Brian. Where's my sister?"

"She's in the next room. She has a broken leg and a big cut on the back of her head. We will take her to surgery soon. She'll be just fine. Now hold still for me so I can see what all you have wrong with you."

"My back hurts real bad and my arm and my leg."

"I think the arm's broken, buddy. It looks like that leg of yours is a little out of whack too. We'll send you to X-ray, and then we'll put a cast on your arm and maybe your leg and check on your back." Turning to another overworked ER nurse, he ordered an MRI and total body X-ray stat for both of the children before turning back to the child. "Be thinking about what color cast you want, Brian. We can do Mickey Mouse, Superman, or Power Ranger or any plain color you like so your friends can write their names on it. I think we have a princess too, but I'm sure you won't want that one. Maybe your sister will. Be ready to tell me before I put it on."

Brian's lip trembled as the pain killers took effect. "I think I'd like a blue one. The guys will like writing on it. Marcy Jones had a pink one when she broke her arm. She got forty-nine names before they cut it off."

"Bet you can get more than fifty. All of us here can sign it before you go home. That will give you a head start on Marcy." Brian smiled through his tears as the sedatives began to take effect.

Jade and Jeff watched as the two children were rolled down the hall toward X-ray. "Let's get a cup of coffee, and I'll tell you what I think we'll need to do for them. They won't be ready for us again for another twenty minutes at least."

Jade watched him from across the cafeteria table. They had never had a quiet half hour together before. He explained carefully what he would need to do if no further broken bones or internal injuries surfaced in the X-rays. A comfortable silence fell between them when he finished telling her what lay ahead. She was surprised when he sat back, fiddled with his coffee cup and said, "You are very beautiful, you know."

Shaken, she finally said, "I don't think much about my looks. Looks have brought me little more than heartache. But thanks anyway."

"How can your looks possibly bring you heartache?" he asked.

She sighed. "Well, all of my life, since eighth grade at least, men have wanted to be seen with me because of how I look. A beautiful woman on a man's arm seems to do something for his ego. I think many men really believe that if they're seen with, or even talking to, a nice-looking woman, everyone will think they've been to bed together. That lifts their estimation of themselves. Of course, ninety percent of the time, the woman wouldn't get near their beds, so all they have to go on is being seen together and few false innuendoes, or outright lies, will convince people they're worthy of a pretty woman's attention. I have grown past wanting to feed a man's ego."

"It surely isn't as bad as all that."

"Tell me, Doctor. How many times have you heard sly comments about some guy being seen with some hot babe, followed by all of the speculation about what they had done together? Please don't try to deny you've heard that going on. I've heard it in the locker room myself."

Ashamed, he said, "You're right. I have. I usually take it for a grain of salt."

"Not many do. They believe everything some man's dirty little mind can create to make himself look good, never mind the truth or the woman's version. It makes me sick. There is more to life than feeding someone's ego."

He had a momentary thought about her older man friend. Was she really having an affair with him, or did he jump to conclusions about them? "You sound bitter, Miss Kennedy."

"Experience is a great teacher, Doctor. I see the ER nurse beckoning for us. They must be done in X-ray."

The sudden flashback of the rage Ted was having at the time of the accident had brought back a flood of forgotten memories for Jade. Ted had been one of those men who bragged about her good looks and his own physical prowess. Often he would make a snide comment that ignited the imaginations of the men around him. Ted would say anything to make other men think he was a real Romeo in bed. I don't really think he was much more than adequate, but he insisted on so many things that would only feed his touchy ego. That was before she found out he had also been feeding his ego with a number of other pretty women.

Memories of embarrassing incidents flooded through her mind as she scrubbed beside Jeff. She was a bit angry with herself for confiding in him like she had. She was also amazed to realize the depth of her bitterness toward men whose shallowness never saw past a pretty face and a skinny body. No wonder so many divorces occurred after a woman gained a few pounds or became involved with two or three kids. They no longer had time to feed the overblown egos of the blustery men they loved, or thought they did. Ted had no patience with the time she spent with Tommy. He wanted her to be able to drop everything and go barhopping with him. When she said no, he became furious and often left the house yelling at her. She had fallen for that in Ted, but she resolved she would not fall for it again.

Jeff glanced at her out of the corner of his eye as they scrubbed. *I'd like to get my hands around the neck of the SOB that made her feel that way. I wonder exactly who he was. She said her husband? She's right. Many men use women to feed their inadequate little egos. What does your own ego say to you, Dr. Davidson? You're under scrutiny too, you know.*

"I'm ready," he announced. "Let's go see what we can do for those kids."

Four hours later, they walked wearily out of the surgical recovery room. Both of their little patients had come through the bone-setting procedures in fine shape. Neither of the two had serious internal injuries. They were awake but groggy.

Jeff and Jade met a pair of very concerned parents in the hallway. Each of them had bandages or fresh wounds on their faces and arms, but both had been dismissed following emergency room first aid. "Are you the Martins?" Jeff asked when he spotted two distraught people standing in the hallway.

"Yes. Where are our kids?"

"They're fine. They're both in recovery. Each has a broken leg, and your son has a broken arm and back pain, plus bumps and bruises. Your daughter had a bad cut on the back of her head. She was unconscious for a while at the scene. Our other surgical team worked with her, so we haven't seen her since her surgery. They stitched up her laceration. Sorry that they had to shave a nice patch on the back of her head. She may want to consider cutting off the rest of her long hair for a while to even it up. They'll both be fine in time. You should be able to see them in about an hour. They'll bring them up to Pediatrics, I think they said 522, as soon as they're both completely out of the anesthesia. Are you two okay?"

"Yes, we're fine other than a few sore spots. The truck hit the back of the car and pushed us off into the ditch." The reality of the situation began to set in for the worried couple. The father was blaming himself for the injuries to his family. "I should have stopped sooner," he groaned. The man suddenly crumbled and began to sob. The woman reached up and patted his shoulder.

"It's all right, Bob. I shouldn't have insisted you kept going. I had heard of white-out conditions, but I didn't believe them. I thought it was only another fifty miles to my folks. I was much too anxious to see them again. I'll have to call them and tell them what happened. I didn't have any idea that snow could keep you from seeing past the windshield. It's as much my fault as yours."

Jade offered, "Come on into the lounge with me. We'll get you a cup of coffee, and I'll show you the room the kids will be moved to. You can nap in the chairs there until they come up. They'll both be fine." As she walked along, she was thinking, *I can say that to them. That's the same thing they told me about Tommy and it's never been fine since the wreck. I'm making it, but it isn't fine.*

The couple followed her down the hall. "I need to call my folks. They will be worried if we don't let them know where we are. I don't know how to tell them the kids have been hurt. Do you have any idea how long before they can be released?" the wife asked Jade.

"I imagine tomorrow if they didn't show signs of any more serious injuries. We will be watching your daughter closely to be sure she doesn't show any sign of a concussion. That was a pretty big cut on the back of her head. I know broken bones aren't fun, but they will feel better in a few days. If I were you, I would worry about getting my car fixed first so you can go on."

"The trucker's insurance company already contacted us. They will pay for a rental car until ours is fixed," Mr. Martin told her. "Our own insurance will help too."

Jeff watched her lead them down the hall. Lucky people. Even if their kids were banged up, they would heal and they would have a family again. Sometimes people weren't so lucky. He turned and walked toward the elevators. At times like this, the failures always came back to him. The times he had to face parents with the news that their child would never be the same or, even worse than that, the times he had to tell them he hadn't been able to do enough and their child was dead. Those were the times when he hated his job.

An hour later, he helped settle the two children in their beds. Both were still groggy but able to talk with the parents. Brian proudly showed off his blue casts. "I think I can have over a hundred kids sign both of them." Brenda had chosen Mickey Mouse for hers. Jeff heard Brian tell Jade, "The baby there had to have a Mickey cast. She doesn't have anyone to sign hers."

Jade laughed at Brian. "I'm sure she'll have a few people. By morning, yours will be ready for everyone to sign. Now it's time for you to get some sleep. If you don't rest, you won't be ready to wake up for breakfast. It'll be coming in about three hours. I hear you get pancakes and scrambled eggs with plenty of syrup and butter." She knew the sedatives would put him to sleep quickly.

Brian went a little pale. "I don't want anything to eat."

Jade smiled at him and brushed his hair back from his eyes. "By morning, you may feel different. If you don't, the nurse can probably find some ice cream whenever you need it. Rest for now, okay?"

"Sure," he said and shut his eyes much too tightly for real sleep.

"I'll see you in a little while," she told the parents. "I have to check on some other patients. They should both sleep for a while. Ring the buzzer if they wake up and need anything," she called to them as she slipped out of the room. The parents nodded gratefully at her.

Jeff met her in the hall. "Thank you, Miss Kennedy. You did a wonderful job for me tonight. Why don't you go down to one of the empty rooms and go to bed for a while? I'm going to sleep in my office. From the sound of the weather report, we will have people straggling in to relieve us all day tomorrow. We need every bit of sleep we can get."

Jade realized that she was very tired following the extended hours. "You're right. I do need some sleep. I'll go to room 506. One of the pipes broke in there last week, and it's closed off. There's a recliner in there, and it's usually quiet too. Did they say if the snow had let up yet?"

"Not yet, the end of the storm is still in Omaha. That could be anywhere from eight to twelve hours from now. This is Iowa for you. You never know what to expect. I've heard that, but this is the first chance I've had to really see it for myself."

"See you later, Doctor." He watched her limp down the hall and disappear into 506. A few minutes later, he jumped when Lisa called to him.

"Doctor, are you all right? You've been standing there gazing into space a long time."

Slightly embarrassed at being caught, he answered, "Yes, Lisa. I'm fine, just tired like everyone else. I'm going to sleep in my office. Call if there's anything you need."

Lisa watched him walk away. His shoulders sagged with weariness, and he moved a bit slower than usual. "He may be tired, but there goes a man in love if I've ever seen one. I wonder if Jade has caught on that the great doctor is in love with her? She's so wrapped up in her nursing and her music and Tommy. I just hope she doesn't let Jeff get away from her. I agree with Maggie. They would be so great together."

Chapter 11

For the next two weeks, Jade practiced on the baby grand at the arts building as often as possible. One late evening, she entered the atrium on the first floor after she finished her shift. One the spur of the moment, she decided to play a while. She practiced a short piece that she planned to use in her senior concert. She preferred the concert grand at the arts building, but they closed at nine. She had access to a piano at her church on weekends, but the one in the atrium was the closest for her. Jeff heard the hauntingly beautiful music floating up through the open areas of the fourth-floor atrium one evening when he stayed late with an emergency surgery. He took the elevator down to first floor, only to find no one there when he arrived. Whoever was playing was very good. He wondered who it could be. Since no one was in sight, he assumed it could even be a recording. *Too bad. I could have used a little relaxing music after this day.*

Maggie met him one afternoon near his office door ten days before Thanksgiving. "Dr. Davidson, I understand that you like classical music."

"Yes, I do. I attend concerts every chance I get. I haven't been to any performances here yet, but I'd like to go next semester. I understand the symphony conductor is doing some great things with the University Symphony."

"He is. If you aren't busy Friday evening, why don't you come with me? There's a special guest pianist in the recital hall. A young woman well known to all of us is returning for a senior concert performance. Several from the hospital are going. I'd be happy to have you go with me. My husband wouldn't be seen at such thing as a concert." She's misleading him a little, but she's not telling him a thing about Jade. Maybe this is a good time for him to learn a few things.

"Maggie, are you asking me for a date?" he teased.

"Good Lord, no and yes, I'm an old married nurse trying to drag an overworked doctor out for an evening of relaxation. My husband and I came to an agreement years ago. I could go to concerts with friends, and he would watch TV alone or with his friends. I thought you might like a break."

His eyes twinkled. "I accept. And I would be pleased to escort you to the concert as a 'friend.'"

"Good, I'll let you know times later. Oh, you might want to know, it's formal."

The week flew by quickly. On Wednesday, the thirty-two student nurses handed in their final ethics paper outlines. Jeff began reading them every spare moment. His plan was to return the papers by Monday morning so the nurses would have his comments on their progress before starting their final papers that would be due at the end of the semester. He knew he wouldn't have a spare moment, but he planned time for the Friday night concert. That one indulgence would allow him a bit of relaxation between papers.

He wondered if Jade would attend. She seemed knowledgeable about classical piano, and she had said she liked music. Most of the CDs she played for Tommy were classical piano. Surely, she would be there. He had hinted at her plans on Wednesday, but she offered no clue to him what she would be doing on Friday night. He had asked her, but her answer had been a vague comment about "plans." He even checked the schedule to see if she was to work. When he saw she wasn't scheduled, he wondered what her other plans consisted of. He felt a little let down when he saw that her name was not on the list for Friday night.

At four o'clock on Wednesday, he began checking papers. Out of habit, he counted them before he started. He was missing one draft. Irritated, he checked his watch. It was a quarter to five. A student had fifteen minutes left to turn in the paper outline. He did not believe in coddling students along at that stage in their education. If they were unable to meet class criteria, they needed to be weeded out. Everyone should have been able to do adequate work of average quality without anyone helping them along. He determined that it was Penny Hansen's paper that was missing. Penny! Even her presence irritated him. Professionally, he could not allow himself to tell her to get lost, even though that was exactly what he wanted to do each time she appeared. Her none-too-subtle hints for meetings and get-togethers were always turned down or put off, but she didn't seem to understand he was simply not interested.

When Penny appeared at four fifty-five, he was angry at her last-minute interruption. "Dr. Davidson, could you check my paper now? I would like to have it before the weekend so I can work on it."

"Sorry, Miss Hansen, I told everyone that I'll have them on Monday morning. That will make it a level playing field."

She looked at him blankly. "What?"

"A level playing field, Miss Hansen. Surely you know that means everyone will have the same amount of time after I give my comments. It keeps everyone even."

"Oh...oh, yes." she said blankly. "I guess that is fairer to everyone. I was just hoping that—"

He picked up his papers and walked away from her. "I'm sorry, Miss Hansen. It will be Monday."

She looked back at him, hoping for a smile of encouragement. Seeing none, she left. *He's such a blind idiot. I've done everything I know of to get him to notice me. How can he be so insensitive?* She walked down the hall, fuming at his lack of cooperation with her dreams and plans. "Jade Kennedy! I just know it's her, but I can't catch them at it. She thinks she's so good. She's got the entire staff wrapped around her little finger with her sob story about her old injuries and her research projects. I don't see what she wants to fool with that idiot Barnes kid so much. I agree with the old Head of Pediatrics. He's a hopeless case anyway."

Jeff had wandered through a number of houses the real estate agent found for him over a two-month period of time. Some were big enough but were too dark inside for his taste. He really didn't like the ultra-modern designs or a house in a suburb where a hundred houses looked nearly alike. He couldn't decide on any of them. He was always drawn back to the large house near the hospital. It wasn't until he found the large five-bedroom property with a guesthouse in the backyard was still available that he was genuinely excited about his own place.

He stood eyeing the guesthouse. It could be a detriment or an asset. He could consider hiring someone to maintain the place for him and allow them to live there. Many male students would jump at a job mowing or blowing snow off the long driveway. Flexible hours and a place to stay for nothing would be appealing. Even though he realized the house was too large for one person, he advised the agent to move forward with the sale as quickly as possible. She told him it wouldn't take long for the house had been on the market for several weeks. She also informed him that the owners would be willing to include the furnishings if he wished. He told her to go ahead and take the furnishings as he had little more than the clothes he wore, a collection of cowboy boots, dozens of country western recordings, and his computer setup.

Chapter 12

On the evening of the concert, Jeff picked up Maggie at her home. She introduced him to her husband Don. Jeff remembered seeing him at the fall picnic and a couple of other times. "I'm glad someone likes this type of thing," Don said as he shook Jeff's hand. "Otherwise, I'd be gussied up in a tuxedo and taken out for a 'night of culture' all too often for my taste. It's the only thing we don't like to do together other than watch sports on TV. This way you two can have a good time, and I'm happy."

Jeff liked the rotund, slightly balding Don. The crinkles of laughter around his eyes matched those around Maggie's. She stood on tiptoe and kissed Don before the two of them walked out the door together.

"What does Don do?" Jeff asked as he held the car door for Maggie.

"He is an electrician. He's a little rough on the edges," Maggie explained. "He's a really good man. I love him to pieces, and I think he likes me too."

"He obviously does, Maggie. I'd like something like that someday."

"Are you looking?"

"Yes, but I can't seem to interest anyone."

"Penny Hanson seems quite available. She's always around," she teased.

"Is she ever? She seems to be borderline stupid in her academic endeavors but dangerous in her hints and innuendoes toward me. She didn't even know what a level playing field meant. How did she make grades for admittance to the nursing program?"

"Don't you know who she is? Her father is the owner of one of the biggest businesses in Des Moines. As an alumnus, he makes huge contributions to the university. There's a program for student relatives of former grads. She came in on that one."

"Hardly seems fair in her case. A more worthy person should have been given the slot. I guess that happens all over the country though. If you've noticed, I avoid her as much as possible."

"I know you do, Jeff, but I think you need to be extra careful. One incident like we had last spring and you could be in big trouble."

"What incident was that?"

"Well, last semester, she managed to arrange a tryst with one of the medical students that put him in a compromising situation. I know they were both students, so the brass didn't care about it. He transferred out at the end of the semester to get away from her, but those things follow you wherever you go."

"Do you think he was guilty or not?"

"Definitely not. If any of the rest of the women around here had thought he was, we would have crucified him."

"Sounds like I need to be extra careful." He quieted as they drove into the parking lot of the auditorium and began to look for a parking space. "Are you up to a short walk in those spiffy heels?"

"They may be spiffy, but they're expensive enough to be comfortable. A nurse has to protect her feet all of the time."

Fifteen minutes later, they entered the auditorium. Their tickets put them three rows back in the center section. "This building is really beautiful," he commented after they sat down. "I was drawn to this university by the advertisements attached to this building. I really should have been here before this."

Jeff was surprised to see several of the student nurses slip in front of them. They all greeted him and Maggie. "Is this the hospital cheering section or what?" he asked her.

"I told you the soloist is someone that we all know. I'm so proud of her I could bust my buttons. I even like to think that I'm a part of the reason for her being in the nursing program."

The orchestra began arriving. They sauntered on the stage carrying instrument cases and music stands, chatting among themselves. Several opened music cases, set up stands, put instruments together, and began warming up.

Individuals tuned with each other. Everyone tuned with a first chair oboe student when she stood and began to give them the pitch. Jeff sat back in his seat, enjoying the warm-up processes. The trill of a flute momentarily floated over the blare of the basses. A drummer played a riff, tightened the drumhead, and played it again. The tympani player played a moment on each of his three instruments and adjusted the screws to his satisfaction. A tuba player blared over the rest. Jeff leafed through the program, reading about the conductor and the first violinists.

There were two students who would trade off as first violinist for the evening. They would gain experience by sitting in the prestigious first chair. He enjoyed violinists playing bits of their favorite passages or practiced a difficult solo section. Instead of hurting his ears, he reveled in the lovely sounds, anticipating the time when they united to begin the concert.

Maggie and the nurses, residents, and interns around him visited quietly among themselves. He only half listened while the tuning continued. At exactly five minutes before eight o'clock, the lights flickered. He tried to read the program but gave up when several people distracted him. Excitement and anticipation hung in the air as late arrivals rushed to get seated before the lights dimmed to cover the audience in darkness. All musicians took their places. A hush fell over the auditorium. Jeff made a quick note that Jade was not among the students around them. It saddened him to think that she would miss a concert. He was sure she would have enjoyed it.

Precisely at eight, the first violinist stepped to the microphone and introduced first the orchestra and then the conductor. Applause greeted the spry conductor as he bounded into place, bowing first to the orchestra and then to the audience. Jeff was stunned to see that it was the man Jade had met in the music building. *She's having an affair with the conductor of the university orchestra! A lot of nerve he has. He's going out with a student nurse. I just read about his wife and family a minute ago. That picture of him must be thirty years old. I didn't recognize him at all.* He was mulling over his outrage at that fact when the maestro took the microphone and raised his hand for quiet.

Jeff half listened as he surveyed the members of the orchestra. "As you all know, tonight is a very special night for all of us, especially our featured soloist. When our dear friend was injured over two years ago, we feared that her career as a concert pianist had come to an end. After a year of extensive physical therapy and a year of extremely hard work, I'm pleased to tell you that she's returning for her senior concert. It's my great pleasure to introduce to you, our own Ms. Kathleen J. Kennedy-Barnes."

The students around him rose to their feet, cheering wildly before Jeff could hear the name of the student. He sat in his seat wondering what was wrong with them. No one received a standing ovation before the concert. Maggie grabbed his arm and pulled him to his feet also. When he stood to his full height, he was shocked to see Jade Kennedy striding across the stage to meet Dr. Taylor. A slim black dress flared around her ankles as she approached the smiling conductor. Dr. Taylor leaned over, kissed her cheek, and turned her to face the audience, Jeff's breath caught in his throat. *My God, she's the most beautiful woman I have ever seen. But this has to be a joke. Kathleen J. Kennedy-Barnes is our Jade Kennedy?*

Suddenly it hit him. If her stage name was Kathleen J. Kennedy-Barnes, why did she use Jade Kennedy? Why had she let him go on believing she was a miss? Then he realized that she had not led him on in any way. Something like the origin of her name had never come up in conversation. Everyone sat down around him. Belatedly, he joined them. What was going on?

He glanced at Maggie's beaming face. Jade was walking to the piano as Dr. Taylor was introducing the first selection. Jeff immediately recognized the strains of the haunting melody he had heard rising through the atrium area at the hospital. It must have been Jade all along. Too stunned to take it all in, he began to listen to the music. Jade was a master pianist. The music drew the audience out of itself, lifted their souls, and played with their emotions before lifting them higher or gently allowing them to float back to reality. Jeff was astonished at the depth of emotion that Jade put into the piano. Not only did she make the instrument talk to the audience, she was able to manipulate their feelings as she played through the score. For three minutes, the audience sat spellbound in the face of great talent.

Jeff sat through a long piece by the orchestra and then another with Jade as soloist. One last short piece brought them to intermission. Jeff turned to Maggie. "Why didn't you tell me?"

"It wasn't my place, Doctor. Jade is very sensitive about her talent. She thought that she might never play again after the car accident broke her left wrist, as well as her left hip. The physical strength was a major concern for so long that she thought she might never play a concert again. She's determined, you know. After the year of therapy, she started practicing again. Dr. Taylor talked her into going for her music degree as soon as he saw that she could hold up long enough physically to do this senior concert. The mental block she suffered took longer than the physical."

Jeff thought back to the day he had seen her meeting with Dr. Taylor. They must have been verifying the date of the concert, not a personal tryst. "Why should she have a mental block?" Then he remembered the night they had worked together during the storm. She had told him that until that moment, she did not recall what had happened at the time of the accident that broke her wrist and hip. She had appeared to be relieved to remember the horrific accident.

"Shhh. They're starting again."

The ritual of introducing the new first violinist and the conductor was repeated before Jade returned once more to the stage for the second half of the concert. Jeff studied her as she walked across the stage. He detected the slightest limp as she turned to seat herself at the piano once again. *So she's had a broken hip. Maybe that was why she appears to be so clumsy. That had to be rough for someone as young as Jade. I wonder why she would have any qualms about returning to the concert stage. She seems to be holding up very well.*

The audience was once again enraptured by the magic quality of Jade's playing. Jeff sat in awe as Jade played long runs of notes that ran together so smoothly they might have been a waterfall. He realized that there was only one more selection from her before the concert was over. He definitely did not want the evening to end.

He thought that he had learned all of the surprise news he could stand when the conductor turned to introduce Jade's last song. "It is with great pleasure that I give you

Kathleen J. Kennedy-Barnes. She will introduce her final selection."

Jade smiled her glowing smile as she took the microphone. "I wish to thank all of my friends who have supported me during my long road back to the concert stage." She paused as the group from the hospital whistled, clapped, and called her name. "It is with pleasure that I play Dvorak's Symphony No. 9 in E Minor, Opus 95, from the New World Symphony. I would like to dedicate it to my son, Tommy Barnes." Thunderous applause followed as she returned the microphone to Dr. Taylor and seated herself at the piano again.

"Her son, Tommy Barnes!" Jeff felt as if he had been hit in the stomach by a prize fighter with a two-by-four. Tommy... Tommy Barnes, the little boy in 512. Why didn't you realize that you fool? Her involvement was not just that of a student nurse. Jade is Tommy's mother! He missed the beautiful first passages of the symphony as he mulled over the news he had just learned. *An automobile accident. Injuries. Tommy's injuries. Oh, my God! Tommy is her son, and I have been chewing her out for not being there. The man who died in the accident was her husband. I have bawled her out for her decisions, her involvement with Tommy, and her sureness about Tommy's case. Even when we worked together, I was too blind to realize that she was talking about Tommy. I have made numerous nasty comments about the mother's absence even as she stood beside me. I questioned her when she said the decision might have been different another time. I'm a total fool. No wonder she's often cool and detached when we talk. No wonder she walks out when I appear. No wonder her face closes into an unreadable mask when I walk up to her. She's waiting for me to lower the boom on her again. How in the world am I going to get myself out of this one? Why hasn't anyone told me?* It hit him then. *Page three of the chart! I have been so stupid. She or someone else has tried a dozen times to tell me to read the chart on Tommy's background and family connections, and I ignored them all. How can I face her after tonight?*

He forced himself to concentrate on her music. She looked pale and fragile as she caressed the keys. The sadness of the piece tugged at his heartstrings. She took them into a peaceful interlude as she played the section of the symphony adapted into River Road. It was the most profoundly moving rendition of Dvorak he had ever heard. He wished it would never end.

As the final strains drifted into silence, the audience sat silently for several seconds before breaking into wild applause. They stood. "Bravos" came from all around him. Piercing whistles and yells of approval filled the air from the student section. Jade had left the stage with Dr. Taylor close on her heels. Three minutes later, as the clapping continued, the conductor returned as the audience remained in place. Jeff couldn't hear the professor's comments as he once again introduced Jade for a short encore. For one last time, she carried them with her on a short emotional ride, ending with a chord of wild abandon.

The final bows were taken by Jade, the conductor, then the orchestra, the conductor again. At last, Jade stood alone. The lights went out except for a single spot. She stood in the glare of the spotlight flushed with triumph at the success of her concert. Long-stemmed red roses were tossed from the audience to the stage in front of her. She stooped to grab a handful and rose again to hold the blood red flowers against the black dress. Her pale skin glowed from her efforts. Jeff thought he had never seen a more beautiful sight. At that moment, he accepted that he might as well face it. He was madly in love with Jade Kennedy.

Chapter 13

He also realized that he had really messed up his chances of winning her as his own. All of the antagonism between them flashed before his eyes as he sat watching her accepting accolades from the audience. Maggie and the others around him were applauding wildly. He joined in but kept watching her closely. She suddenly swayed a bit in the spotlight, bowed one last time, and slipped away into the wings. The stage lights faded out as the curtain closed. The house lights rose as the audience filed out.

Jeff turned to Maggie, his eyes bereft, and asked again, "Why didn't you tell me?"

"I told you, she forbids it. She said you had a lesson to learn. I'll leave it up to her to let you know what that lesson is."

Suddenly, his beeper sounded. He slipped out of his seat and pulled his phone out of his pocket. Maggie stood at his side while he dialed the hospital. It was Penny Hanson. "Yes, Penny, what is it?" The irritation showed in his voice.

"Dr. Davidson, I'm scared. That Barnes kid opened his eyes and looked at me. I don't know if you wanted to know, but I thought it was a big change. He's pretty restless right now. He never moves this much. It's eerie. What should I do?"

"Put on the classical tape by the bedside and hold his hand. Keep him as calm as possible. I'll be there as soon as I can. Observe him closely until I get there. Thank you for calling."

Maggie's face was full of concern. "It's Tommy, isn't it? What's wrong, Jeff?"

"I don't think anything is wrong, but I do need to go check on him. Penny gets a little carried away at times. Oh, do you think you can make up an excuse to bring Jade to the hospital before she goes home? It might help me avoid a confrontation with Penny at this time of night."

"I don't know. Jade's exhausted. Didn't you see her sway just before she went backstage? I couldn't see very well, but I think she was really limping too."

"So do I, but this may be important. I think she should be there."

"I'll get her there. If it isn't anything else, we might keep you out of trouble with Penny. It was something like this that got that intern in trouble. She called him to meet her late at night, then cried rape attempt when he showed up."

"Wow, I'll have to be careful. Can you keep Jade from worrying?"

"Are you kidding me? She'll be frantic. I'll just tell her that I left my safe keys at the desk. She'll understand. I have a history of forgetting keys. She'll go with me to get a moment with Tommy. Can't you tell me anything more?"

"Not yet. I just have a hunch. See you soon." He left as quickly as he could move through the crowd.

Maggie headed for backstage. Jade smiled when she saw her. "Maggie, I knew you would come. It went well, didn't it?"

"Jade, you were sensational."

Dr. Taylor walked up beside Jade. "I've tried to tell her that, but she has to hear it from each of us individually."

"Dr. Taylor, I'm not that vain."

"Well, you should be. It was perfection."

"You know the encore was a little slow."

"I also know you pushed yourself much too hard by choosing that particular piece. It's short, but one of the most difficult and physically taxing you could have chosen. Why didn't you do the sonata we talked about earlier?"

"Adrenaline, I suppose. I just felt so great out there playing. I didn't want to quit, and the feeling was so uplifting. I'm afraid I like the applause a little too much."

Maggie moved up to her. "Jade, I need a ride back to the hospital. Do you think you could take me? You know me. I left my office keys there, and I need to get them before morning. I rode here with someone else, and they had to leave because they were on call. I assumed I could hitch a ride with someone."

"Of course, you know I'll take you. I'm parked just outside the back door."

Dr. Taylor advised her that she should sleep until noon after the trying concert. She laughed and told him, "Well, at least nine. I have to work on my research paper. Dr. Davidson is pushing for me to get at least half of it done in two weeks. I'd like to surprise him and be almost all done instead."

The two women moved slowly through the stragglers of the crowd. People stood around in small groups waiting for orchestra members. Jade spent several minutes with Karen Taylor, the orchestra leader's wife.

"Andrew is so delighted that you were able to pull this off. Andrew has always said that you are the greatest talent he has ever worked with. I think he would adopt you as our third daughter if he could. I do hope you will consider some guest appearances with the Symphony in the future. It wouldn't have to be something so taxing as this concert but short appearances for our enjoyment."

"I'll consider it, Karen. He mentioned that I might want to make a recording too. I could use the pieces from tonight and add a few more for an acceptable disc. Right now, I need to concentrate on completing my nurse's degree. That is taking up all of my time for the next year."

Maggie pulled on her elbow. "Let's get going. Will we see you at the party Sunday evening?" she asked Karen.

"Of course, we'll all be there. I expect over a hundred people. We're planning it in the ballroom of the Union. This is my thing to organize you know. Andy says I'm good at it, and it keeps me out of his hair planning things while his time is taken up with music. We'll see you Sunday evening."

Maggie wanted to scream at Jade to hurry as she lingered with the orchestra members. At last, she moved away from the final group and led Maggie to her car. "I'm really tired, but a good tired, a really triumphant tired, Maggie. I didn't realize how much I needed to follow that dream until I was on the stage."

"We all loved it. I hope you will consider doing guest appearances for Andrew. It might not be a permanent job playing, but it would give you the opportunity to perform occasionally."

Jade laughed. "Tonight I would say never. Tomorrow I'm sure I'll agree."

Ten minutes later, Jade turned into the parking ramp. "Do you want to walk up with me, or do you want to wait here?" Maggie asked her.

"You know me, as long as I can move, I'll go along. I haven't seen Tommy since morning anyway. Have you noticed how much more restless he is lately, Maggie? I wonder if he's in pain."

"Oh, I don't think so. I guess he has been fairly restless, but nothing else seems different."

They reached Fifth floor five minutes later with their long dresses making a swishing sound and their high heels clicking in the near-silent hallway. "I'll just get my keys while you check on Tommy. See you in three," Maggie called as she went on down the hall. She was dying to know what Jeff had learned, but she was determined to leave the telling to him.

Jade slipped into Tommy's room. The symphony was playing quietly on the CD player. She was startled to see Penny by Tommy's bed and Jeff standing beside the bed wearing a tuxedo. If there had been a graceful way to do so, she would have left. He glanced up at her. "Well, Mama. Here you are."

He knows. Oh Lord, he knows. I wonder if he was at the concert. He is dressed up, and does he ever look good in that tux. "Why are you here? What's wrong?"

"Well, I went to a concert tonight, and then I received a page. I answered it."

"A page? Why? Is there something wrong with Tommy?"

"I don't think so. Tommy, look who's here. Here's Mommy."

Jade stared as the little boy opened his eyes and looked at her. "Mommy," he said. He smiled before his eyelids dropped again. Jade swayed. Jeff managed to reach her side in time to catch her as she fainted.

Maggie entered the room. "Well, what's going—" She rushed forward and knelt beside them. "My God, what happened, Jeff? Do we need a code blue?"

"No. She'll be all right in a little while. She just had a shock. Tommy opened his eyes and smiled and called her mommy. She promptly fainted." He shook her gently and called to her. "Jade? Jade, wake up. Come on, babe. Wake up."

She came around enough to realize that she was lying in Jeff's arms, and he had just called her babe. She realized how wonderful she felt in his arms. She lay a moment trying to orient herself. *Why am I lying here in Jeff's arms? What has happened?* She saw Maggie standing by the bed checking on Tommy. His eyes fluttered open again. "Mommy?" he said.

"Did you hear that, Doctor? He just asked for her."

"I heard it. Come on Jade, wake up. Someone's asking for you."

Her eyes flew open as she struggled to get up. A voice was calling her—Mommy? Mommy?—calling so urgently, calling her to wake up. *I must be dreaming. It feels so good to be in his arms. I think it's Jeff, but he's never that gentle with me. Someone is holding me. It feels so good just to be held.* She lay, savoring the feeling of a hard body against the softness of her own. Then she came around enough to realize that Tommy had just come out of his coma long enough to call her mommy.

She realized it really was Jeff holding her, maybe a little too tightly. She could see the concern in his face. "What happened?" she asked groggily.

He smiled at her. "Your son just looked at you, smiled, and called you Mommy. You promptly keeled over on me. He's calling for you now. How do you feel?"

"A little woozy. I really fainted?"

He grinned with relief. "You just fell for me again, right into my arms. I thought you were going to hit the floor before I could get to you, but you chose to go down slowly and gracefully." He smiled at her. "That's the second time you've fallen for me."

Oh my god. I fell for him again. What must he think of me? Tommy, he said Tommy was awake. Her eyes opened wide. "Tommy opened his eyes?"

"Yes, and he just opened them again and asked for you."

"Asked for me? He couldn't possibly remember, could he?" She struggled to get up. Reluctantly, he helped her to her feet. She stepped to the bedside and stared at her son. Tommy turned toward her. His big blue eyes, so like her own, flashed recognition.

"Mommy," he sobbed and reached for her.

She gathered him into her arms. Her tears dripped into his soft blond hair. "Baby, baby. You came back to me. Oh, Tommy. You came back." She turned to Jeff with alarm in her face. "What brought this on? Why do you think he woke up? Can you tell if he's okay?"

"Whoa, let's do one question at a time. I have been suspecting that the restlessness was a sign of something else going on for about three weeks now. I thought he might be in stage three recovery from a coma. I think he woke up because it's God's time. I have absolutely no other explanation for it. We'll give him some time to get used to being awake and then run some tests. I'm amazed that he remembers you. It's been what, two or three years?"

"Two years last March. I need to call my folks. They will be so happy. I suppose I should call Ted's folks too. I'm not sure they will care, but I do think it is the right thing to do."

Jeff watched her as she fussed over Tommy. She was ghostly pale, and he thought she was still swaying a bit on her feet. "Wait until morning. Right now, I'm tempted to enter you into the hospital for exhaustion. You have circles as big as baseballs under your eyes." *But you are so beautiful. I like the updo and the dress.* She seems oblivious to how pretty she really is. I hope Tommy coming around takes away some of the sadness in her eyes.

"Thanks a lot, Doctor. I'm fine. Really, I am. It's just that the concert was tiring and now this. I guess my system is a little overloaded. This is such a shock. I kept telling myself to get prepared for him to get worse or die, but I never thought to prepare myself for this."

"He will probably drift in and out of consciousness for an unknown length of time. Right now, I'd at least like to prescribe that you go home to bed. If he keeps calling for you, you may be very busy for the next few weeks. Try a mild sleeping pill."

"I won't need a sleeping pill. I'm worn-out."

"That's exactly why you need one. You'll start thinking about the success of the concert and Tommy waking up, and you won't sleep a wink. I want to see you in bed until noon and then back here to visit with your son."

"Let me wait until he goes back to sleep," she begged. "He should, you know."

"Yes, I know. That is the usual pattern, awake a little while and then a natural sleep for several hours. That could go on for days or weeks, Jade. You need to prepare yourself for the long haul. We won't know how long it will take before he's ready to return to normal life. You don't need to wear yourself out the first few days. We'll just have to see. At least this is a very good omen for his future." When Tommy had fallen asleep twenty minutes later, Jade and Maggie prepared to leave.

"Is Jeff still here?" Jade asked.

"Yes, he went to his office about ten minutes ago. He said he'd be staying the night so he can be close to Tommy."

Jade knocked on his door. He opened it. He stood there in his suit pants, holding his white shirt in his hand. Her breath caught. *Get a hold of yourself, Jade. Just because you're faced with a half-naked man doesn't mean you have to fall to pieces.* She willed herself to ignore his state of undress. She swallowed a pang of desire as she pulled herself together and began, "Dr. Davidson, I want to thank you for all you've done for Tommy. I had hoped, but I never dreamed he would come out of the coma."

"I hoped too, Jade. He's a tough little boy. I'm afraid I can't take the credit, as much as I'd like to. Someone with more power than I have sent him back to you."

"I prayed for this for so long that I gave up praying. I know it was wrong to give up, but I felt so hopeless."

He wanted to reach out to her but restrained himself. The black dress was low in the front, showing plenty of cleavage. The long black sleeves, and the tight skirt that flared below her knees showed off her slim body perfectly. He wanted nothing more than to take her back into his arms and kiss her until they were both senseless. Taking a deep breath, he told her, "Jade, you really need to go home and get some rest. I know Maggie is tired too."

"Yes, of course she is. Thank you again, Doctor."

She turned to walk out. He called after her. "Jade, I need to talk to you some more about Tommy... I have several ideas I want to try with him. And I need to apologize."

"Don't. I realize you now know about Tommy, but I don't want to talk about it tonight. Let me accept what is happening first. Let me get used to the whole idea, Doctor."

Doctor! I wish to hell you would forget the doctor bit. I want to hear you call me Jeff. I want you to look at me as a man who wants you desperately. I want you to forget all of the terrible things I've said to you over the past few months and learn to love me as I love you. He knew it could not happen the way things were.

She turned and walked over to Maggie. "Let's get going. Tommy's asleep. I'm running on empty, and I know you have to be too. I'll be back tomorrow." None of them realized that Penny Hansen had been standing in the shadows of the hallway for some time watching the three of them for several minutes. Nor did they realize she had taken a small notebook from her pocket and wrote down some notes before going on about her business.

As they walked down the hall, Maggie was telling Jade, "I'll see you about two tomorrow. I can't tell you how happy I am for you, Jade. This is even more than we had expected from this day."

"Actually, it's from yesterday. I see it's past midnight. Let's get to bed."

Jeff watched the two friends walk away, wondering how he was going to get around all of his mistakes with Jade. There had to be a way.

Chapter 14

Jade avoided Jeff for the next two days. Thanksgiving was coming up, and students were excused from duty during the holidays. Jade worked with Maggie as much as possible to be near Tommy. His progress was slow, but there were many hopeful things going on. He smiled when Jade appeared and always reached for her to take him in her arms. The day he cried when she left was considered to be "normal" behavior for a small child. She was the only one he called mommy. They marked it as a milestone the day he recognized Maggie, sobbing Mag-gee, as he held out his arms to her when she started to leave the room. He struggled to sit up, and he played with the stuffed animals placed in his bed. They turned on *Sesame Street* and *Looney Tunes* cartoons for him. He watched and sometimes giggled and pointed toward the TV screen. Occasionally, he babbled. His eyes, so like Jades, sparkled with interest when Jade read him stories

"Jade, how much was he talking when he was injured?" Jeff asked her one afternoon when he managed to corner her in Tommy's room.

"Not a lot. He made singing noises and said mommy and dada, cat, baby, and ball." Tears came to her eyes as she told him about Tommy learning no. "He used it on us whenever he could. I suppose maybe twenty or thirty other words. He especially liked to yell 'cookie.' I was too busy to count them. At the time, I thought he was a genius. Now I know he was just a normal little boy. Do you think he'll ever catch up, Doctor?"

"I don't know. Why not? Aren't you ready to take him home?"

"Yes, but you know me. I'm his mother. I'm prejudiced. I want him to be perfect. I want him to be just like he was before the accident and progress rapidly to the genius level." She smiled ruefully at herself. "As for taking him home, do you think that's possible?"

"I do think he can be discharged if we don't find anything on the tests. I can't promise genius, Jade. I think we can hope for normal unless something unforeseen shows up in the tests we run. We are in uncharted territory. His other physical injuries healed long ago. The daily therapy helped keep his muscles working, but after so long, he has to work on his own." He continued to check the little boy and played idly with him and a toy for a few minutes.

They were both delighted when he threw a toy at them. "He loved to throw things. I know it's a typical little boy trait, but he had so much fun at it. We called it the 'pickup' game." Jeff noted tears in her eyes as she described playing the game.

Jeff looked up at her. She stood watching him with her big blue eyes. "Jade, I really need to talk to you about my behavior."

Her eyes changed to frosty ice. "Forget it, Doctor. You were just doing your job."

"No, I wasn't just doing my job. I was egging you on from the moment I first ran into you in the hallway. I said things about Tommy's mother and didn't even bother to try to find out who she was. I put myself above everyone else by not reading the chart as you and others told me I should."

A tiny smile flickered across her face. "You were a little arrogant about it."

"I was more than a little arrogant. I hurt you, Jade. I didn't know why until the night of the concert."

"The concert? What happened then?"

"That is when it all came to me, or rather slapped me in the face. The fact that you were Kathleen J. Kennedy-Barnes and that you were Tommy's mother was a little over-whelming to me. Then when I realized what an ass I'd been about you, your research, and your attachment to Tommy, I had to ask myself why."

"And did you come to any conclusion?" she asked bitterly.

"Yes. I did it because I wanted you to notice me, Jade. I wanted you to stop presenting me your professional side and turn some of your passion for your research, Tommy, and your nursing career toward me. I saw you with Dr. Taylor once and jumped to false conclusions. I wanted you to laugh with me like you did with Maggie and Lisa. I want you, Jade. I want you to want me not as a doctor to work with and advise you but as a man who is falling in love with you."

Astonished, Jade looked at him for a long time. "Dr. Taylor? His wife Karen and I have been friends for a long time. Andrew is like a second father to me. I don't understand why you would think there was something between us." Finally she drew a deep breath. "I think I'd better go, Doctor. You know how I feel about the ethics of a nursing-student-doctor relationship. I don't think we should discuss this any further. Good night, Doctor." He saw the glint of tears in her eyes as she turned and ran.

"Jade, please wait." He saw Jade bump into Penny Hansen as she ran out. Penny appeared in the doorway of his office. "What do you need?" he snapped curtly.

"Oh, nothing," she said blithely. "I was just passing by when Ms. Kennedy about knocked me down," she said as she walked on, a sly smile on her face as she fished a little notebook out of her pocket as she moved on down the hall.

By the time he extricated himself from Penny, Jade had disappeared down the corridor. He turned back into his office and sat down in the chair by his desk and dropped his head into his hands. *That is the lesson, buddy. You were too arrogant, too pushy, too full of yourself; and now, she doesn't want anything to do with you. How are you going to deal with this situation?* He remembered the fun they had at the picnic. *Test your professionalism. Try to keep your distance even though you want to take her in your arms every time you get near her. Keep your distance so you can't catch that elusive scent she wears. The best you can do is sit near Tommy's bed and dream about having her for your own. Live with this torture. You brought it on yourself.*

Early the next morning, Maggie stepped to the door of Jeff's office. "Are you all right, Doctor?"

"Yes...no, Maggie, I'm not." He sighed. "I'm not sure if I ever will be. I've fallen in love with Jade, and she doesn't want anything to do with me. Why is my whole life going down the drain since I met Jade? I've never had this type of problem before. But then I've never been in love before either."

"Don't give up, Jeff. I think she cares for you, but you do know that she doesn't believe in students and doctors getting mixed up in affairs. And she is a little leery of a new relationship after that husband of hers. He really took her for a ride and made her pretty gun shy. Just give her some space. She'll be graduating in May, won't she?"

"Yes, I won't do anything to stop her graduation. In fact, I wouldn't be surprised if she doesn't graduate with honors. Just tell me how I'm supposed to get through the next semester."

"One day at a time, Jeff. That's all you can do. One thing that will make it easier is that she will be in Geriatric rotation next semester. She'll only be here to see Tommy. That will make it a lot easier for you to avoid seeing her."

"I don't suppose you would consider helping me a little along the way."

"Helping you win Jade? Not a chance, Doctor. I'm no matchmaker. You got yourself into this, now figure out a way to get out of it." She started out before turning back toward him, "Oh, by the way, have you thought of an apology?"

"I just did. That is when she walked out on me."

"Well, the only other thing I can think of is prayer. Good luck. I'll even add a few for you."

"Thanks a lot, Maggie. I'm afraid it will take more than you and me to get her to come around."

"Let's start Thursday. It's Thanksgiving Day. Both of you are committed to eating Thanksgiving dinner with Don and I. I'm having three student nurses and two interns that can't get home for the day or don't have families or live so far away they can't get home so you won't be staring at each other all day. I'll plan on seeing you there with offering in hand at 11:30. It was cranberry salad you mentioned, wasn't it? No excuses accepted."

"Are you sure she'll be there?" he asked hopefully.

"No, but you have to eat anyway."

Maggie talked with Jade Thanksgiving eve. "Are you coming for dinner tomorrow? We'll eat at twelve."

"I don't know, Maggie. I should spend more time with Tommy."

"He's still sleeping a lot. You can see him in the morning, and you'll have all evening to be with him, and you have to eat." She moved some charts on the rack before she asked, "Is it because of Jeff?"

"I won't try to lie to you, Maggie. Yes, it is. I don't know how to take him anymore. Before I could rage and fight with him. Now, I don't know how to react. First, I want to wallow in front of him in gratitude over Tommy's improvement. Then I want to kill him for being so dense all along and expecting me to forget it all. It didn't help any that we had such a good time at the picnic. He even had the nerve to tell me he has fallen in love with me. I can't imagine a relationship with a faculty member."

"Oh, honey, be careful. This is pretty overwhelming to him. Jade, I do believe he loves you."

"Loves me? Oh, Maggie, are you sure? It would be disaster if he does. I keep finding myself drawn to him like no other man I've ever known. Common sense tells me I can't feel anything for Jeff while my feelings tell me that I do. Now you say he loves me."

"Yes, I think he does."

"No, I don't think that's true, Maggie. I know he said so, but I can't think that's true. I don't believe in such relationships. There are too many complications such as jealousy among the other nurses. What would Penny Hanson say if she thought I was after him? You know how she treated everyone over that intern last year. Not to say the complications to my life and his. I don't have time for affairs, Maggie. I have to keep all of this on a professional level. I don't want to think about such a thing, let alone talk about it."

"Okay, I'll let it drop, but I do expect you at 11:45 tomorrow. I'm counting on you for the pumpkin pies and whipped cream."

"All right, I'll be there. I ordered two pies yesterday. How would I explain to Lori if I didn't go to your house to eat?" She tried for a laugh, but it sounded hollow to both of them.

Chapter 15

Jeff was thoroughly ensconced in the living room in front of the TV with Don and one of the interns when Jade arrived at ten minutes before twelve. She handed Maggie a box with two pumpkin pies and a pint of whipping cream. "I don't know if this is traditional at your house, but my grandmother always served pumpkin pies with real whipped cream on Thanksgiving. It and the candied sweet potatoes make the meal as far as I'm concerned. By the way, what is that delicious smell?"

"It's probably my date cake. It will be perfect with the whipped cream too—the real stuff, of course."

Don appeared in the doorway with a big smile on his face. "My Maggie, she never serves anything artificial." He patted his large overhanging belly. "That's why I look like this. How much longer, love?"

"About fifteen minutes. We girls have to finish setting the tables and putting the things on the buffet. Sorry, everyone, you have to fill your own plate. The tables are too far apart to pass things from one to another." She began ordering the nurses and one of the female interns to set the tables, pour drinks, and set serving dishes on the buffet in order: first the plates, then silverware and napkins, followed by space for the turkey, dressing, mashed potatoes, and two dishes of turkey gravy. They set out three kinds of vegetables and hot rolls. Jade set the pies and the date cake on the kitchen pass through with the whipped cream in a bowl of ice between them. Each table held a small platter of pickles, beets, deviled eggs, carrots, radishes, and celery, along with salt and peppers. Don arrived in the kitchen door with a large platter of turkey. Within minutes, everyone was eating.

Jeff could just see Jade from his place in the living room. Jade had chosen a table in the dining room where she sat with her back to him. He couldn't see her face, but the stiffness of her back told him that she was really upset with him. It was hard to pretend interest in the football game, harder still to discuss some serious concerns with the three interns and to keep his eyes off Jade's back.

When he slipped behind her to get dessert, she straightened and shifted slightly away from him. *Damn, this is going to be a lot harder than I thought. She's really giving me the cold shoulder. I know she doesn't want a relationship, but how can I stand this coldness? Oh, Lord, I need some help with this one. I've messed up something awful this time, and I don't know how to get myself out of it.* He had just finished his dinner when his beeper went off. He stepped to the phone to call the hospital.

"Yes, I'll be right there?"

He turned to see Jade's eyes questioning him. "It's an accident case, three kids in a little car hit by a van. At least two need surgery. Dr. Benson is on his way along with the rest of the OR crews. Maggie, I'm sorry to run, but duty calls. Thanks for dinner. It was delicious. See you all later. Happy Thanksgiving," he called, hoping that Jade had heard all he said.

Jade watched him go. She was relieved that it wasn't Tommy. She hated to hear about the little accident victims. She knew the heartaches involved for everyone. She visited with the other women for a while, helped clean up the tables, and put the dishes in the dishwasher and made her goodbyes. "I'm going to go to the hospital to sit with Tommy a while, Maggie. I plan to go home and turn in early. I made a lot of progress on my paper yesterday, and I want to work on it some more tonight. I'll see you tomorrow afternoon." She accepted a hug from Maggie and a pat on the back from Don. "Thanks for dinner. I'm sure I'll waddle around for a week after all that."

Maggie watched her go. Don slid his arm around her shoulders. "How is your little chicken getting along, Hon?"

"I don't know, Don. I think the two of them love each other, but they both have a lot of baggage to get over. He had a lesson to learn about bedside manners and she's fighting her ethical beliefs. It'll be a tough five months ahead. Let's go watch the rest of that football game. The gang in there is half asleep from all of the food. Maybe some of them will hang around for a light supper. I need to get rid of the turkey and the leftovers."

"I hope they do. I don't want to eat them for the next week." She patted his protruding belly. "I feel so sorry for you, chubby."

He kissed her soundly before leading her into the living room. "Make way for the cook and me. We are here to claim the sofa." Everyone laughed but moved quickly to allow them to sit down side by side holding hands. No one seemed to notice that Jade and Jeff were missing.

At the hospital, Jade noticed the silence on Fifth floor. Patients who were able were sent home to their parents for the holiday weekend. The nurses moved quietly about their duties. Jade found Tommy sleeping. She turned on the CD and settled in the recliner for a nap. She woke up when Tommy stirred. He grinned at her and threw the stuffed giraffe Maggie had given him on the floor. Jade played the pick-up game with him for a few minutes before he became tired again and lay back down to sleep. She determined to go home and get more rest and gather her research information for her appointment with Jeff the next morning.

Jeff arrived at his office at nine the next day. Jade had made an appointment to meet with him about her research at ten o'clock. He had no idea whether she would show up or not and even less of an idea what to say to her if she did. Finally, he decided to keep the meeting strictly confined to the research project and see how things went from there.

Jade arrived promptly for her appointment with Jeff. She stuck her head in the door and asked, "Is our meeting still on, Doctor?"

"Of course, I've been waiting to see this paper for a long time."

She spread papers out on the desk in front of him. "The first pile is all of the introductory work. There's the title page, table of contents, forward, etc. The next piles are the major divisions of the paper. As you can see, there are four of them. The introductory information explains the types of injuries each child suffered, the study format, and the various types of music from classical to rock and roll and western. The next section covers the research procedures used, the next the findings to date, and the last pile covers my conclusions. The bibliography and index are in the final pile."

He looked through each pile approvingly. Her organization, writing, and conclusions were excellent. It was obvious that she had carefully planned a firstclass research project. After watching her with the children, he knew she had made a valid hypothesis. "This is very good, Jade. Without a doubt, you can convince the medical world to use your methods for post-surgical and comatose children. I just hope staffs can tolerate some of the rock and roll and hard-rock fans. The music of the last five years would wake the dead or kill the living. I'd like to take a little time and read through all of this right now, but I'm behind on the ethic's class outlines. I've promised them by Monday as you know. By the way, I have read yours and found it very interesting also. Your point is well taken. I'd like to give it to you now, but I've refused to hand out any of the others, so I really can't do that."

"I understand. I don't need it before anyone else. I'll spend the rest of the holiday break on the research paper and do the ethics paper next week. Since the concert is done, I'll have a lot more free time. And now that Tommy is awake, I want to be here with him as much as possible."

"Jade, I haven't told you how wonderful I thought the concert was. You have a great talent there. It must have taken a great deal of effort to come back like you did."

"Thank you, Doctor." She looked uncomfortable. Finally, she stood and said, "I really should be checking on Tommy. He's waking up more often now. I'd like to keep track of his progress as much as possible. I'm considering a paper on the stages he goes through in his recovery."

"If you need some help, please let me know. By the way, may I have a copy of your research project? I can proof it for you and make more suggestions if you'd like."

"Of course, I'll get you one Monday. I could leave this one, but I've already begun to make revisions and notes all over it. It won't take long to run out a clean copy for you. Maybe we will agree on some of the things it needs."

"Jade, I need to talk to you about Tommy."

"Please don't, Doctor. I'll bring my paper to you Monday." She turned and left the office, her papers in hand. He sat staring at the door for a long time before gathering his papers and stuffing them into his briefcase. He left ten minutes later without saying a word to anyone. Neither of them noticed Penny Hansen watching them go or glancing at her watch as they parted.

Maggie watched him stomping down the hall ten minutes after Jade left, his cowboy boots clicking on the floor. "I feel sorry for him in a way. He wouldn't allow himself to do anything someone else hinted, and now he's in this mess with Jade. She's right though. It would be no good for them to have a relationship with her in school and him on staff. I just hope they can last for five more months. They're so right for each other."

Chapter 16

Once classes resumed the following Monday, there were only three and a half weeks left until Christmas. Jade managed to avoid Jeff most of the time. Her two papers were going well and the final for orthopedics promised to be an easy one, at least as easy as a graduate level final could be. She timed her visits to Tommy to miss the hours Jeff would be in his office or making rounds. They met only twice in his room. Each time, she was relieved when he didn't mention anything personal. They were able to discuss Tommy's progress quite rationally. Once, he asked her if she had taken any notes for the paper on his progress. She informed him that she had.

One late afternoon, Jade was in Tommy's room playing with him. She looked up in surprise when Jeff entered the room. Tommy gave one look at him and began to grin. "Eff. Eff. See me," he called as he ran to Jeff and held his arms up to be held. Jeff's heart melted as he reached down and picked him up. He hadn't known how wonderful it felt to have a child hug him.

"Hey, Buddy, how are you doing today?"

"I fine," Tommy said and hugged Jeff as hard as he could. He immediately began to wiggle to be put down to play.

"I think this guy is ready to start eating on his own. Once he masters that, I will have to release him. Insurance doesn't like to keep paying when there isn't a good reason. With the tube out, Tommy will only be looking at rehab services for the next several months. He might be eligible to attend the state school for the handicapped for the first year while he catches up. I've been watching him daily. I think he is progressing at a great rate." He watched Tommy for a few minutes while the little boy played with the toys in his bed. It was only a short time before he flipped over on his side and fell asleep. Jade realized that the two of them had been standing together for some time observing him. It almost felt like they were a couple watching their own child.

Stop that, Jade, she told herself. *You know you can't fall for Jeff. He's your superior here, and he can keep you from graduating if you don't watch yourself.* "I think I had better go. Maggie will be wondering what happened to me. I need to help with the new surgical patient in 542."

"Before you go, I'd like to schedule the tube removal for the day after tomorrow. I think he's ready for it."

"So soon? Are you sure? What if he can't eat on his own? What will we have to do then?" she asked anxiously.

He smiled. "I don't see any reason to delay it any longer. I have been watching, and he chews on some things like he was eating it. I know kids chew on everything when they're around two, but he acts like he could eat. There isn't any other way to find out. Let's see what he does. If he can't adapt, we'll think of something else to try."

Jade took a deep breath. "I guess I'm having a little trouble accepting that so many normal things are happening so quickly. I didn't plan for all of this quite so soon. With the tube out, he will have to be released. I think I have a lot of preparation to do. Wait until I tell my folks." She left the room quickly.

He watched her go. *I can't imagine what she's thinking. She keeps such tight control over her emotions. I hate the way she will be laughing with the nurses and the other men around the hospital and then clam up and turn cold when I come along. I know I was wrong, but I need a break. I just need a glimmer of hope.*

She walked quickly down the hall. *I have to get away from him. It's all I can do to keep from throwing myself into his arms and begging him to love me. Every time I get a whiff of his Obsession, I go weak in the knees. I'm no better than Penny Hanson. I want him, but it can't possibly work for us. I have to keep away from him. I can't deal with a relationship right now.*

Finally, it was the end of the semester. Jade and the rest of the ethics students handed in their papers on the final Wednesday of classes. As they started out the door, Jeff called to her, "Ms. Kennedy? May I have a moment?"

What now? I thought I was going to be through with him for a while. "Yes, is there a problem with my paper?"

"Not at all. I was preparing for my next semester of classes, and I wanted to ask you if you would consider being a guest lecturer for me? I have the 'Medical Ethics in life-and-death decisions' class scheduled, and I would like for you to give your views to the class. Your paper outline was excellent, and there were at least three points that would have a much larger impact on others than anything I can say. You've been through the decision-making and realize the complications. I don't know how you are feeling now that Tommy is conscious. But a lecture on the emergency room atmosphere, the later legal implications, and your thoughts during the time Tommy was comatose would be most helpful. I could schedule you for three lectures if you would do them. I can even pay you a guest speaker's stipend."

She was stunned. It was a wonderful opportunity for any student. It would look great on her résumé, and it would do wonderful things for her bank account too. Still she hesitated, "I'm not sure, Dr. Davidson. I've never lectured before, and I'm not very good at public speaking. I've not been in front of an audience other that my classes since freshman English class."

"It would be helpful to me, and I'm sure the students need to hear from someone who's been through it. Please think about it, and let me know before January 1."

"I'll think about it. It would be good experience for me." She turned to leave.

He stopped her with a quick question. "Is your schedule set for the next semester?"

She hesitated and turned back toward him. "Yes. I have three classes and clinical in Geriatrics. The classes are all two-hour courses, so I won't have as much outside work as this semester. I won't be doing a senior music concert in the middle of everything else, so it should be an easier semester for me."

"Too bad, I would like to hear you play again." He hesitated a moment before asking, "Jade, we talked about sending Tommy home soon. Do you have anyone to take care of him?"

"Not yet. Once I know for sure he's being released, I will have to find a place for us. I don't know how much help I will have to have while I finish this semester." Neither of them saw Penny Hansen walking down the hallway. Even though she attempted to hear what they were saying, all she could hear clearly was him asking Jade to join him for Christmas dinner as she hurried on.

"I won't be able to take the time to go back to my folks. The cafeteria is closed, but there must be somewhere within the area that stays open for those of us who have nowhere to go."

She stood for several seconds before she answered. "No, Doctor, I won't go somewhere with you. You have to know how I feel by now. I would invite you to come to our house for Christmas dinner though. We're having Maggie and Don and a couple of other couples who can't get home for the day. A group thing would be fine."

He expelled the breath he had been holding. "Then I'll accept. What can I bring?"

"Nothing. Just come about eleven. We'll have an appetizer or two and some mulled cider and eggnog."

"Thank you, Jade. I'd like that." He watched her leave. *A group thing, I'll have to accept a group thing for now. It's sure a lot better than a solid no.*

Chapter 17

The Christmas holiday blew in on an icy cold wind that chilled to the bone. Jeff went downtown and purchased a down-filled, knee-length jacket the day before the break. He complained to Maggie. "Why did no one warn me about this weather? I don't think it ever got this cold in Oklahoma. I may be asking myself why I made the move."

Maggie laughed. "It's typical. It's Iowa. Don't be surprised if you can go without your coat one day in January and get caught in a twenty-below blizzard the next day. If you wait a day or two and it will change again."

Jade was astonished to receive a summons from the Dean of nursing two days before the holiday was to begin. "Miss Kennedy, I need to warn you that I have had a complaint that you and Dr. Davidson are having an affair. You are well aware that the university does not condone such relationships. I would ask you to restrain yourself or you will be in danger of being expelled before you finish your degree. It would not be good for the department if word gets out on this."

"I can assure you, Doctor, that there is nothing going on between Dr. Davidson and me. Whatever relationship you are referring to is purely business. He is my mentor on my thesis, and we meet occasionally to discuss the progress of my sick son. You should be well aware that Tommy has been in a coma for nearly two years now. I can assure you that I will make sure there will be nothing for anyone to be suspicious about in the future. I am well aware that such liaisons are forbidden."

"Good. I want you to know if there is any hint of illicit behavior, I will be forced to act on it. I trust that you can tell Dr. Davidson this information. I would call him, but I'm leaving town in an hour or two for the holiday."

"I'll do that," Jade told him as she hurried away. *You pompous ass. You call me in and threaten me with expulsion and to tell Jeff. You coward. You're afraid to tell Jeff yourself.* Still fuming, she headed toward Pediatrics. It suddenly hit her. Who would watch them and draw such conclusions about their…their what? She admitted to herself that she would like to be able to call it a relationship or even a friendship, but their professional situation stood in the way. She would have to tell Jeff that they must be very careful, or she would lose her career over something that didn't exist, at least not while she was still in school.

Christmas day was cold, but the sunshine allowed Jeff's spirits to lift a bit as he hurried up the walk to Lori and Jade's apartment. He noticed the signs of poverty around the building. There were piles of grills, bicycles, and items normally stored in garages sitting in front of some of the doors. Dead weeds showed in the sidewalk cracks. Older cars and pickups sat in the parking spaces. Some of the apartments had flag or sheet drapes. All signs of a lack of money. It was a typical college housing unit. He assumed that a lot of students lived in the building because it was cheap and a temporary place to stay while they studied or partied. He hoped it was safe for the two nursing students.

He rang the bell and waited for someone to let him in. He carried a large bag of small packages filled with essential items anyone could use and two bottles of wine. In his pocket was a special gift for Jade. He hoped to get a moment of quiet opportunity to give it to her.

Lori answered the door. "Dr. Davidson, come in out of the cold. We are happy to have you join us." She led him down a short hallway to the tiny sparsely furnished living room. "Let me take your coat and that bag. I'll put it under the tree if it's what I think it is."

"Please call me Jeff out of the hospital. The bag only has a few tokens for everyone to share. I didn't know for sure who would be here." He walked back in the living room to find Maggie and Don stomping snow off their snow boots. The chatter that followed soon set him at ease. He was concerned when he couldn't see Jade in the little group of people.

Jade came barging through the front door a few minutes later. Her cheeks were rosy from the cold. "Brrrr." She shivered. "It's terrible out there." She called, "Merry Christmas everyone," as she headed for a back room to shed her coat. Jeff's eyes followed her every move. *God, she's beautiful,* he thought as she moved into the kitchen.

Maggie cornered him before lunch and told him, "You can't hide it, can you?"

He looked at Maggie. "What do you mean?"

"You are crazy about Jade. It shows on your face every time you look at her. Have you been able to make any headway with her?"

He smiled ruefully. "Not a bit. I do understand that she is concerned about student and faculty relationships causing her problems, but I would appreciate a little niceness until after she graduates in May. After that, Maggie, I intend to pursue my plans to get her to like me."

"Be patient, Jeff. You may have a chance with her. She's still got a lot on her plate. She will have to decide where she wants to work and what she will be able to do with Tommy. She tells me that you are making progress with his rehabilitation programs. I don't know what she'll do when she can take him home."

He looked around the tiny apartment. "I can see that she doesn't have much room here. Her bedroom can't be big enough to add a youth bed or even a crib. Tommy needs a lot more room than this to learn to get around."

Maggie laughed. "Kids adapt. Plenty of them grow up in this complex. Some couples even have two or three kids. I think they must hang beds from the ceilings to accommodate one more little one. So you think it will be soon?"

"I'm thinking no more than another month. I should be able to justify that much more time to the insurance company before they insist we turn him out of the hospital. They usually approve of outpatient rehab services. Do you think Jade will be able to afford a larger place? I don't see anything on the tests to indicate that we should keep him in the hospital much longer. As soon as he starts eating a little better on his own, I'll be releasing him. I thought maybe she could take him home with a full-time sitter, but looking around this tiny little apartment and the neighborhood tells me she can't manage him here."

"That will be a problem for her." Maggie sighed. "She got stuck with the bills from the wreck. Ted's parents have plenty of money, but they blamed her for their son's unhappiness and irresponsibility. He was the driver, but they think she had to cause the accident. They refused to help her with any expenses, even the funeral."

"I wish I could help her."

"I doubt she would accept it from you. Perhaps if you go through me, you might get something done to help her."

Just then, Lori stepped to the door and interrupted their discussion. She called, "Dinner's ready. Come and get it." From that moment on, there was cheerful chatter among the guests while they ate a delicious meal. Jeff sat with one of the young interns and a couple he knew by sight. After the lunch leftovers were cleared, Jeff announced that he had brought a grab bag of items to share. Much laughter followed as men opened wrapped shaving creams, razors, deodorants and soaps on a rope. For the women, he had found perfumes, Chap Sticks, and expensive lotions. They were such simple items, but the recipients of each seemed to appreciate his offerings. It gave Jeff a good feeling when they thanked him.

Two hours later, the couples slipped off for their apartments, each with a plate of leftovers. Maggie and Don left so he could get in a short nap before they started preparing for their children's visit the following weekend. Jeff rose and looked for Jade.

She was in the kitchen, washing a few dishes. "Jade, I'd like to thank you for asking me to come today. It's been very nice. I brought you a little something if you'll take it."

She looked at the small package in his hand. "Jeff, I...I don't think my taking anything from you would be wise. I have been assigned to tell you that I was called in by the Dean a couple of days ago. He warned me that there is a rumor going around that you and I have a thing going. I haven't traced the rumor yet, but I suspect Penny Hansen. From some things the Dean told me, she would be the first one to have access to the information."

He ran his hand through his hair in frustration. "Oh God, I'm sorry, Jade." He paced the tiny kitchen. Finally, he turned to her. "What do you think we should do?"

She looked at him sadly. "Stay away from each other. Don't go near Tommy's room together. Don't call me into your office about my thesis. Don't come near me. Call me on the phone if you have business about my lecturing next semester or about Tommy. By the way, I will help you with the lectures. It will be great experience for me."

"I suppose you're right. We will have to stay away from each other. It will be easier when you move to your next rotation. We can do our business about Tommy with witnesses all the time. If I see you with Tommy, I will not go in the room with you, and we can discuss his case at the nurse's station."

"I'm too close to achieving my degree to take any chances. I can't let anything get in the way. I hope you can understand that." Her eyes pleaded as she finished the last of the dishes and walked out on him. He placed the fancy wrapped bottle of expensive perfume on the kitchen counter, wondering why he felt such anger and so let down.

Chapter 18

Jeff spent the slow days between Christmas and New Year's going over student papers. He gave Jade an A for her excellent work. He almost threw Penny Hansen's poorly done paper in the waste basket before he had an idea. Something about her information seemed very familiar to him and a couple of the quotes were in common use. On a whim, he opened his internet and searched by topic. Within minutes, he had located the published paper from a famous professor. Penny had directly quoted pages from a well-known scientist without giving proper credit for the ideas. He compared the remainder of the paper to the famous publication. The entire paper was a copy. He could not find one original thought in the whole thing. To be fair, he searched through the pages one more time before marking an F in the upper right corner. He wasn't sure why, but he went to his printer and made a copy of the poor work. He didn't like such blatant plagiarism.

Jeff returned the checked papers the first day after the holiday break. He was aware that Penny had turned white and jammed her paper into a notebook case before stomping out of the auditorium. Several came forward to discuss their work with him. He wanted to congratulate Jade on her success but restrained himself from approaching her. Lori gave him a thumbs up as she and Jade left the room.

The second semester started in the second week in January. The weather remained bitterly cold as students hurried across the hilly campus to settle into the new classes. Jeff called Jade several times to arrange the dates and contents of her lectures. Each time he kept it on a business level. He hoped she would say something personal, but it didn't happen.

He stared out the window of his office during the first January snowstorm. He could barely see the row of large old houses south of the campus. He had met with the real estate agent before Thanksgiving and signed all of the papers to purchase the property he had loved. He had moved into his house the first week in December and was getting used to going home to the over large house whenever he had a spare weekend and during the evenings. He liked the house, but it still seemed very big and empty. He longed for Jade and Tommy to live there with him, but he still had no opportunity to court her and tell her he wanted them to be a family.

Jade threw herself into her new classes and her rotation in Geriatrics. She barely remembered her grandparents from either side. As she worked with the patients, she realized just how much she had missed. She continued to spend as much time with Tommy as possible during the hours she wasn't in class or on the Geriatrics floor.

She hurried to Tommy's room between classes early one afternoon. She was amazed to see Jeff sitting on the floor with Tommy and a male rehab assistant.

They were allowing the little boy to walk between them. Tommy squealed with delight. She could hear him yelling "Bubba" as he turned to the assistant and "Eff" as he turned and proudly walked to Jeff. Each time he threw himself into Jeff's arms when he reached him. Jade wiped tears from her eyes as she turned and walked away to keep from disturbing their game.

Maggie saw her coming down the hall. "Well, hello, stranger. How's it going for you this semester?"

"Good. My classes aren't nearly as demanding as some I've had. I like Geriatrics, but I don't think I will concentrate in that area. I plan to apply in Obstetrics when I start looking for work." She watched Maggie working for a while. "Maggie, have you seen Jeff in Tommy's room much?"

"Yes, he goes in there a lot. I think the two of them are bonding pretty well. Jeff has told me he didn't realize how rewarding it was to have a child coming to you so willingly. As a doctor, most of his little patients are afraid of his white coat. Tommy is getting past the hurting tests and finding that "Eff" is someone he can play with. They do have fun together. I've heard the two of them laughing several times lately."

"I guess I should be grateful that Jeff is spending so much time with him, but I'm afraid I'm a little jealous of Tommy's love for him. Tommy was out of it for so long that I would like to think I'm the center of his world."

"It won't hurt either of them, Jade. I see them getting along well. The doctor needs to learn a new side to kids, and Tommy needs a man in his life." She hesitated before adding, "So do you, dear."

Jade laughed bitterly. "I know you're right, Maggie, but circumstances are against us. If I pursue my dreams, I have to stay away from Jeff. I just have to."

"It won't be forever. It's only a few weeks until you graduate."

"In the meantime, Jeff says he will be releasing Tommy. You know we don't have room for him at the apartment. I have to take time and find us some place to live. I have an appointment with a campus housing office next week, but they haven't given me much hope of finding something. Everything is taken up by students. If I was married, I might qualify for a two-bedroom apartment in one of the university complexes for the summer or next fall. All I can hope to find is a private house somewhere near the hospital so I can catch a bus or walk. Hopefully I will have a few more weeks before Tommy goes home. I saw where one of the married men has a wife who wants to take on one child for extra income. I suppose I could manage to borrow enough to get through the semester paying a sitter."

Jade called her parents and told them about Tommy's progress. She had notified them and Ted's parents as soon as Tommy had regained consciousness. "He's doing so well," she told Maggie. "Dr. Davidson is preparing to release him soon. I have to find a place for us soon."

"Oh, honey, I'm so happy for you. I told your brother and sister about Tommy's progress too. We want to come see you soon. We'll get a motel so you won't have to worry about where to put us. Let me talk to all of them, and we'll let you know. I want it to be in the next week or two." They chatted for another twenty minutes before they hung up.

Jade stared at her phone for a long time after they ended the call, thinking how fortunate she was that her parents were behind her all the way. Her brother had always been her defender and her sister her biggest rival. She got excited to think about a visit from them.

Her parents and brother and sister drove the two hundred miles to visit two weeks later. "Jade, you know you need to find somewhere you can live with room enough to take care of Tommy. Your father and I have talked it over. We are ready to sell our house and move to a smaller place. We could take some time and come care for Tommy until you complete your degree and get a job to keep the two of you. We would love to be his live-in sitters if you'll have us."

"If I'll have you? Oh, Mom, that would be so wonderful. Are you sure Daddy's ready for that?"

"It will give us both something to look forward to. You know Dan and Linda's kids are getting bigger, and they live so far away. We would like a chance to be a part of Tommy's life. Why don't you look for some place big enough for all of us? We'll be glad to help you with the expenses of a bigger place."

The three of them looked all over the city for a larger place for them. There were a couple of poor choices. One had a number of stairs, and one was in bad shape with uneven floors. Jade could see college students living there happily, but Tommy needed level surfaces and fewer steps. Her folks and siblings left on Sunday afternoon. They had not found a place for them to move.

Jade called Maggie that evening. "Guess what? My folks are coming to help me take care of Tommy when he's released. Now I have to find an apartment or house big enough for four of us instead of just the two of us. We looked all weekend, but there isn't much available at this time. I may have to struggle along until the students leave town in May, but Jeff talks like Tommy will be released well before that."

"That could be a problem for you. So many places aren't available until June or so. Do you think Tommy will be released before that?" Maggie asked.

"Dr. Davidson says he can't justify keeping him much longer. The tests are not showing any permanent damage. Tommy will need a lot of therapy and some special help catching up, but I can do the therapy. And my mom's a retired teacher so he can get a lot of help from them. Dad is one of those outdoor people who can take Tommy out on walks and play with him. I only have one more semester, and I'll be able to get a job. Keep your ears open for an apartment."

Jeff had wandered over his backyard, kicking a small snowdrift in front of him. He examined the winter trees and bushes and wondered what they would be when they came out in the spring. He walked around the swing set and covered sandbox, thinking that they would be wonderful for some kid to play in. The guesthouse stood empty and forlorn at the west edge of the property. He had paid little attention to it before. His main interest had been on the house. The realtor had advised that it was in good condition and would make a lovely place for a student gardener or several students who needed community housing.

As he wandered over the grounds, an idea came to him. Jade and Tommy were going to need a place to stay soon, for he intended to release the little boy within the next few weeks. It suddenly hit him that the house might be perfect for Jade and a nanny. The upstairs could be a sanctuary for a nanny. Tommy would have the big backyard to run and play. He could offer them a place to stay for nothing. He didn't need additional income from the property. *A place to stay for nothing? I could let Jade move here with Tommy rent free. If I could talk her into living there, I could help her without bothering her.* I have to talk to Maggie and see what she thinks.

He stepped in the back door of the big house and took the cottage keys down from a holder and headed for the guesthouse. As he stepped in the little cottage, he knew immediately that he was going to offer it to Jade. He hoped that she would accept it. It was sparsely furnished but had plenty of room for two adults and one little boy. There were two bedrooms upstairs and one large one downstairs with a large walk-in closet that could be used as a child's room. Now he had to convince Jade that he had the perfect place for her. Hopefully Maggie would help him.

He approached Maggie with his idea. "You know I bought a property near the hospital. I've thought about it all weekend. It has a guesthouse, Maggie. You said you might help me with Jade. I am going to need you to convince her to come live in my guesthouse so she will have plenty of room to take Tommy home with her and to keep a nanny. I would have to struggle to leave her alone if she was that close, but I could manage. What do you think, Maggie?"

"I think it's a great idea. You will be interested to know her folks are coming to help her, so she'll need plenty of room and no need for a nanny. I know she has been worrying about living accommodations for them if you do release Tommy. Lori and her boyfriend are getting pretty serious. They could use a little privacy too. Let me think on this one, Jeff. I could convince myself to help you with that idea."

A week later, Maggie and Jade accidentally met in the cafeteria. They sat down to have lunch. "I sure miss you in Pediatrics, Jade. It's so quiet. How's it going this semester?" Maggie asked her.

"Oh, Maggie, I miss you and Lisa so much. I like the new rotation in Geriatrics though. The other classes don't take too much of my time. Tommy takes up the rest of it. He's making great progress. Every day he does something new. You should hear him talking. He's playing more like a three or four-year-old now. That's tremendous progress."

She picked at her salad a few moments before saying, "Speaking of Tommy, Jeff tells me he will be released soon. I'm going to have to look for a bigger place to move to. I do have one bit of good news. My parents' house has sold, and they have agreed to move up here with me for a while until I can get things set up for Tommy. They will keep him during the day for me and be there in case I have to take a night shift when I start working. I hear they hire a lot of the students for the night shift just to help them get their foot in the door. I hope I can be one of them. It's just that it's so hard to find a place. The housing center can't offer me much closer than forty miles away. I would have to use

Dad's car every day if I took something that far out, and I don't want them stranded with no car."

Maggie felt a bit guilty as she presented Jade with Jeff's idea. "I think I just heard of a guesthouse that will be available for someone to live in soon. I think it would be ideal for you, especially if you folks are coming to help you. You might not like the idea." She hesitated before adding, "It belongs to Jeff Davidson."

Jade looked at Maggie as if she were a traitor. "Maggie, I'm trying to avoid Dr. Davidson. I couldn't live on his property."

"At least consider it. It's a guesthouse in the back of his house. It's only about three blocks from the hospital. I think you can see it out his office window. He says he doesn't want just anyone living there. He might be willing to let you and your parents and Tommy live there. It has a beautiful backyard with some playground equipment out back. If your dad likes to garden or putter around outside, he could even work for Jeff."

Jade thought about Maggie's comment for a few minutes. "Dad would love that. He kept the yard at home by himself. Mom likes flowers, but he took care of them for her. I know he would be able to mow and keep up a lawn even if it is a little large. It is so close to Dr. Davidson. I'm not sure if I want that, Maggie."

"You wouldn't have to see him, and it would be convenient for you. It's really pretty big for a guesthouse. He says it has three bedrooms. That would be perfect for the four of you. Think about it, Jade. I don't think he'll charge much for it."

"Maggie, I can't take advantage of him like that. It sounds great, and it would solve a lot of my problems. Let me think on it. Now, I have to go. I'm scheduled for class in fifteen minutes."

Maggie reported to Jeff the next morning when he arrived for work. "Do you think she'll go along with our plan?" he asked.

"I think it will solve too many problems for her to turn it down. Housing is so tight here in this college town that your offer will be the best she can find, especially on such short notice. I do think you will get further if you charge her for a little rent and her utilities. She needs to feel she's paying her own way. By the way, I think you might have allies in her parents too. They have been pretty worried about Jade since the accident. They didn't have much to help her along, but they are willing to do what they can now that they are retiring."

"I hope this solves our problems," he told her as he moved toward his office.

"I think there is one thing you can do to help her make up her mind fast."

"What's that?"

"Offer the house, then tell her you're going to release Tommy in one week. She will be forced to take you up on the offer. It's a bit underhanded, but it might work for you. I, for one, hope so."

He grinned. "Maggie, you're a genius. She won't like it, but she will have to make a decision right away." She watched him practically dance down the hallway.

Chapter 19

Jade finally approached Maggie two days later. "Maggie, I'm so torn. I have to find somewhere to move ASAP. Dr. Davidson says he's going to release Tommy in a week. My parents can be here by then if I need them. I really don't want to, but I need to look into that house of his if it's still available. I have to have someplace to put us all."

"It will solve a lot of your problems. Do you want me to ask him when we can see it?"

"We? Oh, Maggie, will you go with me? That would be so good. I wouldn't have to face him alone."

"Sure. Just tell me when he will let us in," Maggie told her. As Jade walked away, Maggie smiled. Maybe she could be a matchmaker after all.

Jeff agreed to show them the house the next evening. Jade and Maggie arrived at the guesthouse at the appointed time. Jeff opened the door for them. "I think you will like this place. You had better take it. It will be great for Tommy. He can have his own room downstairs and the run of my backyard. The playground equipment will be good for him too."

Jade knew immediately that she wanted the little house for her parents and Tommy. She still had reservations about being so close to Jeff, but she was desperate for a place for all of them to live. There was the big bedroom on the ground floor, plus a living room, dining room, kitchen, and bath. Upstairs there were two large rooms and a bath. Jade could imagine her parents using the two rooms for themselves and their privacy whenever she was free. Tommy could be kept downstairs. She could envision making the big walk-in closet into a space for Tommy. She was so excited at the prospect that she wiped a tear from her eye as she drove back to the hospital. "Oh, Maggie, it's perfect for us. The only thing that bothers me is the closeness to Jeff. I hope he keeps his distance."

"I think he will. He knows that is the wisest thing to do," Maggie assured her.

The next morning, Jade advised Jeff that she would rent the house for the token three hundred dollars and utilities. He hated to accept it but knew that it would be better for everyone if she maintained her pride. "I think you should move in as soon as possible," Jeff told her. "I'm planning on releasing Tommy in a few days. If you and your parents get moved in, I'll help furnish the house for you. Some of the furniture there is pretty old and shabby, but it's serviceable. Let me take care of the moving bill too."

"You don't have to do that, Doctor. The folks are bringing a truck load of their most valuable things rather than put them in storage. Dad has a pickup that he'll be bringing, as well as their car. I'll visit the used stores and find what we need."

Jade made arrangements with Jeff and her parents to move them in the next weekend. Tommy would join them a few days later. She took Maggie shopping with her two days before they were to move. "I need a bed for Tommy, a kitchen table, and chairs and some recliners. The little TV at the apartment is mine. I'll put it upstairs for Dad and let him put his bigger one in the living room. I'd like to find a stand for it. My dad will be watching Westerns and sports most of the time. I don't have a lot of money to invest in furniture. I'll use my bed and dresser from the apartment and my recliner. Look for a little dresser I can use in Tommy's room. Everything else in the apartment is Lori's."

They browsed through the stores, looking for items she could use in the house. "Oh look, Maggie. I love this little table. It will be great with a nice big reading lamp for Mom. I think I'll let Mom and Dad pick out what they want upstairs. They arrive tomorrow, you know. I can hardly wait. They can move into the house immediately, and I'll move my things on the weekend. Tommy is due to be released on Tuesday." She stopped and wiped a tear from her eye. "I thought it would never happen, and now it is only a few days away."

Jade and her mother worked to prepare the big closet for Tommy. Between the two of them, they managed to paint the little room a sunny yellow. Jade was delighted to find a large clown decal to put on the wall near the bed area. It was large enough for a youth bed, a dresser, and a large toy box Jade found in the used store. When they were all ready for Tommy to come home, Jade sat on her bed and cried, "Oh, Mom, I wasn't sure that I would ever get to this day. He is actually coming home."

Jade attended her class on Tuesday morning and then hurried to Pediatrics to meet her parents. They were waiting in Tommy's room for her to arrive. Tommy was dressed to go out. Tears filled her eyes when she saw him in the little overalls and polo shirt with sneakers on his feet that her mom had chosen. The staff on Fifth floor had gotten him a new coat with matching mittens and hat. She bundled him into the coat, savoring the moment of normalcy. When he was dressed, she hugged him close as the tears ran down her face. "Mama cry?" he asked.

"Yes, Mama cry. Mama cry because she' so happy you are going home with her today."

"Om," he muttered.

"Yes, baby, home."

Maggie came to the door. "Jade, I need you to sign the release papers." Jade signed the papers quickly with one shaking hand while Tommy clung to her other side.

"Thanks, Maggie. I can't tell you how much I appreciate all you've done over the months Tommy has been here." Jeff was standing at the nurses' desk when they walked by.

"I see someone is going home today," Jeff commented as they walked up the corridor. Tommy squealed, "Eff. Eff," and reached for him. Jade reluctantly let him move over to Jeff. She jumped back when she brushed against Jeff. Jeff tried to ignore the electricity between them as he took the little boy and held him close while Tommy sat contentedly in his arms. When he tried to move Tommy back to Jade, the little boy began to cry and cling to him even tighter.

They stood looking helplessly at each other as Tommy continued to cling to Eff. "I guess I'll have to carry him to the car for you," Jeff finally said. "He doesn't seem to want to let go."

"I can see that. Dad is supposed to be parked near the south door." The two of them walked along together through the long hallway to the elevators with Maggie and Wilma walking behind them, laden with toys and equipment. Tommy clung to Jeff in fear when the elevator began to move. Jade silently thanked heaven that the elevator was smooth and quiet in its descent. Tommy still clung to Jeff. When they reached the outside door, Jeff again tried to transfer Tommy to Jade's arms.

"Come on, Buddy. Mommy will help you." Tommy finally let go of Jeff and dived into Jade's arms as they stood waiting for John to drive up in the car. "It's a great day for you, isn't it?" Jeff asked to break the uneasy silence between them.

"Yes, it's one I hadn't truly prepared myself for. I can't tell you how great this feels. I need to thank you for your interest in Tommy. I know you helped him recover by spending all that time with him. Oh, here comes Dad. We'll see if I can remember how to get a kid in a car seat."

Maggie, Lisa, and two other student nurses stood on the curb to wave a goodbye to Tommy. He watched them with eyes full of curiosity. Maggie finally told Jade, "Don't go on about it, or I will start bawling. Just give me a hug, and get out of here. Remember I'm going to retire soon, and I will be upset if you don't call me to give everyone a break. I intend to be number two sitter."

Tommy looked around him, wide-eyed and curious as Jade carried him outdoors. He did not want to let go of Jade long enough to be strapped into the car seat. Jeff watched helplessly as she literally crawled into the car and hung onto him while her dad helped fasten the straps from the other side. He whimpered when she pulled away to fasten her own belt.

His whimpers turned to screams when John started the car. "Oh, Tommy, it's all right, baby. You don't think he remembers the accident, do you, Dad?" she asked when John and Wilma were seated in the front seat.

"It's hard to tell, honey. I used to think a kid couldn't remember anything until they were five years old, but I distinctly remember falling into the water tank when I was not quite two and having someone pull me out by my overall straps. I also remember seeing my sister tossed off her pony and landing on the corner of the chicken house. Later, they told me I was just twenty-six months old when that happened. They weren't things I tried to bring up. They were just there. He may remember the wreck too. It would have been pretty traumatic for him at the time."

Jeff stood dejectedly watching them leave. He told himself it didn't matter that there was still an empty seat on the other side of Tommy. He could have filled it quite nicely. He waved toward the car. He couldn't believe how good it felt to have Tommy turn around and wave back. The good feeling stayed with him as he headed back to Fifth floor.

"You can't imagine what a great day this is for Jade," Maggie told Jeff as they walked back to the elevators. "She has worried that Tommy would never come out of the coma. It didn't seem like it would ever happen."

Tommy began to quiet down as they moved out into traffic, but he refused to let go of Jade's hand. She was thankful that it was only a short drive to Jeff's house. The little boy continued to stare at things as she unfastened the seat belts and lifted him back into her arms. For the next hour, the three adults watched the tiny boy as he acquainted himself with his new surroundings. He struggled to walk and often fell to the floor to crawl. Jeff had assured them that he should be able to walk on his own as soon as the muscles gained strength. John and Wilma had been given a crash course in physical therapy techniques that would help Tommy's progress. They fed him a light dinner and put him in the gleaming white youth bed Jade had found at the used store. He turned over on his stomach and promptly fell asleep.

Jade stood watching him sleep. She hadn't been sure this day would ever come. As she watched the sleeping child, she thanked God and Jeff Davidson for giving him back to her.

Chapter 20

Jade was so happy to have Tommy home with her. The first few hours had been like a dream. Tommy played with John after she dressed him in his pajamas for bed. Amazingly, he slept most of the night, waking only once for a drink of water. She left the next morning before he was awake. Wilma and John were waiting for him to wake up. Jade knew they had a full day planned. They had talked about walks, swings, sandboxes, and what to feed a growing boy. Jade left for work, assured that Tommy was well taken care of.

That evening, John and Wilma had Tommy calling them Papa and Nana by the time Jade came home from the hospital. "That's another good sign, Mom. He learns very quickly."

She was not prepared when a stranger approached her the next day with a sheaf of papers in his hand as she left her shift at the hospital. "Are you Kathleen J. Kennedy-Barnes?" he asked.

"Yes, I am." She assumed he was someone who knew she used her entire name for music department business. "How may I help you?" she asked politely.

"Here," he shoved the papers into her hand. "You've been served," as he turned and walked away. Jade stood staring after him before glancing at the papers. She nearly fainted as she read the title "Custody Suit."

Jade stood in the hallway, leafing frantically through the sheaf of papers. Words popped out at her: Unfit? Neglectful? Harold and Clarice Barnes, Ted's parents, were claiming that they would be best for the child. They were the ones who had abandoned the unconscious child. They were the ones who had called him a vegetable and advised that they wanted nothing to do with him. They were the ones who had literally abandoned him for months. They were the ones who had not contacted Jade for updates since they walked out of the hospital two months after he became unconscious.

Now they were alleging that they deserved Tommy because he was their dead son's legacy. They wanted total custody with no undue influence from the mother of the child. They claimed that she was incompetent and could not provide monetarily as they could. Jade imagined that they could be successful in their suit for they had enough money to buy any lawyer they wanted. She hurried to the nurse's lounge and fell into a chair before she began to sob.

The supervisor of Geriatrics found her ten minutes later. Jade showed her the papers. "My in-laws are filing for custody of my little boy. I can't provide money for him like they can. I'm so afraid they can use their money to get their way." Jade began to sob.

The supervisor stood beside her for a few minutes. "Is there someone I can call for you?" she finally asked. "Perhaps you should take the rest of the day off."

Jade dried her eyes and shook her head. "No, I'll be all right. I would appreciate the day off," she answered as she began to control herself. "I can get to Fifth floor by myself. Don't worry about me." She walked in a daze to Pediatrics. Maggie looked up from the desk and immediately rose to meet her.

"What is wrong, Jade? You look like you've seen a ghost."

"Oh, Maggie, the Barneses have sued me for custody of Tommy." She slapped the papers down on the desk between them. "They claim I'm unfit to raise him. They want him now because he is Ted's legacy. I don't know what to do." She sobbed. "I don't know how I can afford to fight them."

Jeff came out of his office at that moment. "What's wrong?" he asked, his eyes full of concern.

Without saying a word, Maggie shoved the papers toward him. He picked them up and glanced at them before beginning to read them word for word. "What the hell makes these people think they can take Tommy away from you?"

"Money. They never accepted that Ted had married a poor student who was beneath their social standards. I'm so scared," Jade told them. "They have all the money in the world to get what they want."

Jeff frowned. "Come into my office. I'm going to make a couple of calls."

Jade followed him blindly. Penny watched from down the hall as they entered Jeff's office. Hatred filled her eyes as she watched Jade. She took a small notebook out of her pocket and made a quick note before moving on to perform her duties, making sure she could see Jeff's door to note the time Jade left his office.

Jeff called the campus lawyer, Jason Tedrow, and pressed speaker on his phone so Jade could hear their conversation. "Jason, this is Jeff Davidson at the hospital. I have a student here that has a custody suit thrown at her. What can we do? Yes, she is a student. Her son was a patient here in a coma for almost two years. Now that he has come out of the coma, the paternal grandparents are suing her for full custody. They have the money to back their request. She's still a student."

"Let me look into this. I don't know if it will fall under the university legal department, but I can find someone who can take the case. Boy, what kind of people are they?"

"I don't even want to say. I can testify that they had no interest in the child as long as he was comatose. Now that he's recovering, they are claiming they have a father's rights to him. The mom is scared to death."

"Tell her to hang in there. We can surely win this case for her."

Jason called Jeff the next day. "I've been talking to Dr. Dean Black, head of the law department. He is an extremely good lawyer, as well as professor. He says the law department takes on a case for their students each spring. He was delighted to think that they could go to court against someone like the Barneses representatives. Take down the professor's number and give him a call. You may have the entire senior law class representing your friend."

Jade and Jeff met with four senior law students and the professor the next day. "We will need a copy of Tommy's medical records," they were told. "Also, give us a listing of all of the money the Barneses gave toward the child's medical bills and the number of times they visited the hospital to be with him."

"They didn't even provide a dime to the funeral expenses stating that I was responsible for the accident and my husband's expenses. They didn't pay one cent for Tommy's care. They visited once after Tommy was hospitalized, and it is charted that they came once after he came out of the coma. They only stayed a few minutes both times. Their attitude in the beginning was that they wanted nothing to do with a 'vegetable.' I wasn't aware that they had been to see him recently until after they were gone." Tears rolled uncontrolled down her face. "Can you keep them from taking him from me?" she pleaded.

"We think so. Let's gather all of the information you have. We've been looking into grandparent's rights. Some states have them, and some don't. It will be very hard for them to take a child away from his mother, especially under these circumstances. They might be able to get visitation rights here in Iowa since your husband is dead. Do you think you could handle that?" he asked Jade.

"I will if I have to. Could it be supervised? I don't think they would ever hurt Tommy, but they could afford to take him out of the country before I knew he was gone. It's just that I am pretty bitter toward them after they left me with all the expenses and their attitude toward Tommy. I'm still paying on part of them."

They visited for another hour before Jeff and Jade left the office. "We'll discuss everything and get back to you in a few days," Professor Black told them as they left.

Outside, the sun was shining brightly. The fresh winter air stung their nostrils as they walked back to the hospital. Jade didn't say a word. Finally, Jeff broke the silence, "Jade, you do realize that the whole hospital staff on Fifth floor will be willing to testify. Maggie has been there as long as Tommy and Lisa were there prior to that. They can be your star witnesses."

"I know. It's just that I hate to ask that of them. They've been so good to me. Now I'm drawing them into this dirty business." She began to cry. "It isn't fair, Doctor. It isn't fair."

In spite of himself, Jeff reached out and took her in his arms for a moment. It was all he could offer for comfort. *God, she feels good in my arms. I'd like to keep her here forever.* She clung to him for a moment before straightening and pushing away from him. "Sorry," she said through her tears. "I shouldn't have done that. Thank you for going with me today. I'll be in touch," she called as she hurried away. From the Fifth floor, a pair of angry eyes watched them break apart.

Chapter 21

M aggie stopped Jeff two days later. "Are you busy tomorrow evening?"

"Not that I know of. I don't have anything scheduled. Guess that makes me a dull person. What did you have in mind?"

"It's Jade's birthday. She'll be thirty. Her folks and some of her friends plan to surprise her with a party tomorrow night. I thought maybe you would like to come."

"I'd like that. Can I bring anything?" he asked.

"Sure, your favorite ice cream. I hear Jade likes butter pecan. We'll have vanilla and strawberry for her too."

"I'll be there when?"

"Seven."

Jade and her mother were in the kitchen, talking about Tommy when a knock sounded at the side door. Jade opened it to find Jeff standing outside with a bag draped over his arm and two large boxes in his hands.

"What is this?" she asked, slightly irritated that he had broken his promise to keep away from them.

"Happy Birthday, Miss Kennedy. I brought food and presents."

"So you brought food and presents? How did you know it was my birthday? I've already gotten the best present possible."

"A little birdie told me. I knew you didn't seem completely happy with the decisions I made for you the other day. And I thought perhaps birthday cake, ice cream, and presents would help a little. I know I pushed you to take the house, but I thought it would solve your problems. I also read page three of the chart. That was what I should have done a long time ago. Page three of the chart told me what was happening."

"Oh, Jeff, you didn't need to do that. I was only put out because things were happening so fast, and you had the perfect solution before I even had a chance to think about it. Cake, ice cream, and presents are certainly most welcome. Let me help you with them." She took the cake and ice cream and turned toward the freezer. She was totally aware of the male hardness of his muscles and the smell of the Obsession hung around him. She chastised herself a bit when she realized her gut reaction to his presence.

"Here, Mom, put this ice cream away until we're ready to eat it. Tommy should be awake soon, and I'll open this gift and then serve the cake and ice cream. I don't want him to miss it."

Jeff stood just inside the door, waiting. At last, Jade became aware that he was still standing there. "Come on in. You might as well join the party if you have time. After all, you did bring the food and the present."

"He didn't bring all of the presents," John boasted. He stood in the living room door with three large packages in his hands.

"And I brought a few more." Lori and Jack stuck their heads around the corner.

"And I brought some ice cream toppings and more packages." Maggie laughed as she and Don came up behind John.

Jade smiled at them all. "I guess this is the time to yell 'surprise.'" They obliged her.

Wilma fixed coffee, and the eight of them sat in the tiny living room visiting until Tommy called, "Mama?" Jade hurried in to pick him up and change him before presenting him to the room full of adults. He smiled and held out his arms to Maggie. "Mag-ee."

"Yes, sir. It's Mag-ee. How are you doing, big fella?" She took him and moved to the living room where the others waited.

No one was prepared when Tommy screamed "Eff!" and reached for him to take him. Even when they began serving the treats, Tommy refused to be taken from Jeff's lap. Jade noted that the two of them seemed perfectly content in each other's company. She felt a pang of envy that she was not, could not, be included in their cozy little world.

She watched as Jeff shared his desserts with Tommy. He wiped the sticky ice cream toppings from Tommy's chin a bit awkwardly. Jade noted that he was very gently with the wiggly little boy. She also knew that feeding a child might not be in Jeff's area of expertise. He handled sick children all the time, but a healthy little boy was something entirely different. She smiled as she watched them.

When the women picked up the plates and forks, Tommy spied the pile of packages on the coffee table. "Box, box," he cried and reached for them.

"Come on and help Mama open her birthday packages. Don't forget that you are the best birthday present she could ever have," Wilma told Tommy as he climbed down from Jeff's lap and reached for the packages. Jade picked him up and set him on her lap while she tore into the gift wrap. Jeff watched Jade open her gifts. Several of them were gag gifts designed to make everyone laugh at her advanced age of thirty.

"You're over the hill now that you're thirty. Old age approaches, dear," Wilma warned her.

"Mom, that's years away. I know I believed life was over at thirty when I was a teenager, but I did learn enough to know it has just begun."

Jeff had given her two tickets to the upcoming London Ballet fall season performance at the auditorium with the hope that she would ask him to attend with him, a pediatric reference book he knew she couldn't afford, and a bottle of White Diamonds perfume. She had thanked him politely, exactly as she had thanked everyone else. By nine o'clock, everyone had filled up on ice cream and cake.

Jeff could see the purple shadows under her eyes. "I think it's time for me to go home," he announced. "Jade has had a very long day, and we haven't a clue how Tommy will adjust to these new surroundings. I'll see everyone later." He left through the dining room and let himself out the front door.

"We had better go too, Don. Jeff is right. It's great, but it has been a long day. Give me a birthday hug, Jade, and we'll be on our way." They noticed Jeff walking slowly toward the back door of the main house, his shoulders slumped against the chilly wind.

"I feel a bit sorry for him," Maggie told Don. "He is head over heels in love with Jade, and she keeps him at arm's length. I hope things slow down and work out for them. Maybe after she graduates, things will change for them."

Lori just hugged her. No other words were needed. "I'll see you tomorrow in class. Get some sleep, Mama."

"Thanks, everyone. It was nice. Just being here with all of you has made it a perfect day. Jeff was right. I'm beat, and I really do hope Tommy sleeps at least part of the night. So far, he has the schedule of a two year old. I'll be so happy when he sleeps all night and is potty trained. Mom is working on that."

The days flew by. Tommy made rapid progress under the watchful eye of Wilma and John by day, and Jade at night. They all rejoiced as he began to run in the yard. The potty training progressed rapidly. Occasionally Jeff would slip by after work and watch Tommy's progress before Jade returned from work. He and Tommy continued to play together. It was a milestone when Tommy finally called him "Jeff," but he missed having the child chase after him yelling, "Eff, Eff!" He was totally taken aback when Tommy called him "Dada" one afternoon when he was pushing him in the swing. He didn't tell anyone that had happened, but he treasured the moment.

Both Wilma and John noticed that Jade and Jeff were avoiding each other. "Oh, my. I thought maybe…once they were together in a more relaxed atmosphere. But now, they seem further apart than ever," Wilma told John a week later.

"No use speculating about it, Wilma. You know how Jade feels about attachments between faculty and students. I just hope he doesn't give up too soon. I wouldn't mind having him for a son-in-law."

Chapter 22

Jade's lectures were scheduled for the last week of February and the first two weeks in March. She was very nervous before the first class. The weekend before she spoke on Wednesday, she reviewed her notes with Lori for the third time. "This is so hard, Lori. I hope no one thinks I'm a real authority on any of this. So many of the ideas I have would be helpful to those who have to make snap decisions. I keep thinking how wrong I would have been if Tommy hadn't come out of his coma. Where would I be if it hadn't worked out this way?"

"Jade, you can't dwell on that. You would have done your best if you had to face a permanent disability. Right now, you need to worry about getting your point across. We in the medical profession do need to be brutally honest with people are faced with making difficult decisions like you were facing when they brought you in to emergency."

"That's my main point. Maybe we aren't brutal enough. If someone had said, 'Your son will be a vegetable,' would I have begged for them to save him? Would I still have him today?"

"Of course, you would have. You're his mother."

"What if they did say that to me, and I was too out of it to listen?"

Lori scolded her before the lectures. "Come on, Jade, be realistic. You are pushing honesty and truth. You know every person takes the same news differently. You're telling medical personnel what they need to do. You took 'could be' and 'might be' to 'possibly' and turned it into 'hope.' There are never any guarantees any given decision would ever fit the next case. You have great ideas. Present them and see what happens."

"You're right, girlfriend. I'm just a little overwhelmed by the awesome responsibility of the whole thing. I don't want to let Jeff down either."

"You'll do just fine. That, I can guarantee."

Jade laughed. "Thanks for the vote of confidence."

Jeff arrived at his office late on Thursday afternoon after a long day of emergency surgery. A legal envelope lay on top of his daily correspondence. Slowly he opened it and began to read. A frown developed across his brow as he read. He wiped a hand over his eyes and read it again before picking up the phone and dialing the hospital administrator's direct line.

"Phil? Jeff Davidson here. We've got a problem. We have a lawsuit filed against us by a student nurse."

"What the hell? Why?"

"A student nurse is alleging that she's been discriminated against by faculty, she's been treated unfairly by fellow students, and I have sexually harassed her."

"What the hell are you talking about? Do you have any idea what you just said?"

"Of course, I do. None of it is true, but I know what something like this can do to a school, let alone to a man's career."

"How much?"

"Ten million."

"Ten million! Where did she get that kind of a figure?"

"It's apparently what she thinks she would make in a forty-year career if she graduated."

"Cripes, what's her major? Surgery? Radiology or what?"

"Nursing."

"Nursing! Do nurses make that much?"

"Some make half that if they are very specialized in heart or transplant assistance. She's also asking for half of it for pain and anguish."

"Shoot. What information can you get about all of this?"

"Plenty, I'll ask for reports from several nurses on the floor outlining her negligence. Her coursework speaks for itself. It's slipshod work at best with a lot of provable plagiarism. She approaches me every chance she gets. I never felt like I encouraged her in any way. I have some witnesses to a lot of that."

"Look, let me set up a meeting with LeRoy Carlson. I'll call with a time tomorrow morning."

"I'm scheduled for surgery at 6:00, 8:30, and 10:00. It's hard to cancel this late."

"Make it one then, my office. I'll get LeRoy out of anything he has going on."

"Good, I'll be there."

"Bring every bit of ammunition you have. I've got a feeling we're going to need it all. And whatever you do, be discrete about this. We don't want this leaking out any sooner than we have to."

"One more thing," Jeff added. "She's naming another student in the suit."

"Another student? Who's that?"

"Jade Kennedy."

"Our piano playing Jade?"

"Yes."

"Good Lord! Why her?"

"Miss Hansen is claiming alienation of affection."

"That's 1940s Hollywood. Whose affection anyway?"

Jeff's voice went flat. "Mine."

"Yours!"

"Don't yell, Phil. I already have a headache over this whole thing. Yes, mine. Penny is alleging that she and I were on the way to the altar until Jade came in and stole me away from her. I've never had a date or anything more with Miss Hansen or with Miss Kennedy."

"What makes her think there is something between you and Jade?"

Jeff took a deep breath. "I'm in love with her, but I don't know how she feels about me. She has avoided any hint of a relationship because of the student-faculty taboos. There's nothing between us because she won't let there be until she gets her degree in May. I'm waiting for her to finish. I'm not sure what Penny thinks she has on us other than that."

"Oh, hell. That does it. Bring Jade along. This is more complicated by the minute. You'd better have some good evidence and a lot of support if we beat this thing."

"Phil?"

"Yes?"

"Please keep your mouth shut. Jade doesn't love me back. Penny must have sensed my feelings, but Jade doesn't acknowledge me that way at all."

"That's all I can deal with at one time. Both of you be here at 1:00 tomorrow," he lamented. "I should have retired months ago."

They hung up. "I should have too," he groaned. Now he knew how Jade must have felt when she received the custody papers.

Just what I need, another lawsuit to be involved in. Talk about a mess. My life seems to be going down the drain fast. First, I can't have the woman I want and now this. What was it, Jade said, "It isn't fair." What about Jade? She already has one lawsuit on her plate and now this. I certainly hope it doesn't break her. What a damn mess. He sat at his desk, staring at nothing for several minutes before reaching for the phone to dial Jade's number. Wilma answered. "Wilma, is Jade there?"

"Yes, who's this?"

"It's Jeff."

"Oh Jeff, I don't think she'll talk to you."

"She has to. Both of our careers are at stake."

Jeff could almost hear her hesitation. She finally said, "I'll get her."

After a long pause, Jade answered, "Hello."

"Jade, this is Jeff. I have bad news. Penny is suing me and the university and naming you as an accomplice. We need to meet with Phil Thomas at one o'clock tomorrow afternoon. Please be there. We'll try to sort it all out then," he rushed on, afraid she might hang up on him.

"I don't understand. How can she do that?"

"You know how spiteful she is. It isn't hard for her at all."

"All right, I'll have to rearrange my schedule, but I'll be there."

"Thanks."

She hung up. *Damn, damn, damn, damn. Just what I need, another lawsuit. I never liked Penny, but I never dreamed she would do something like this. I hate to admit that I am drawn to Jeff, but I can't let anything happen between us as long as I am in school. Maybe after I graduate, I can look at our situation again.*

He cradled the receiver for a moment before slowly setting it down. He wanted to scream, yell, throw, or hit something. His father's voice echoed in his brain. "Big boys don't cry," but he wanted to. He gathered up some paperwork and left the hospital to walk the three blocks to his house.

Chapter 23

The next afternoon, Jeff and Phil met in the hallway outside the attorney's office. Jade was not in sight. "Where is your friend, Jeff?"

"I don't know, Phil. I told you she will not have anything to do with me although she did say she would be here."

"She better be. We have to plan a strategy to beat this thing. I hope your feelings don't show when she's around. That will make it harder on all of us."

Five minutes later, the two men glanced up at the sound of the elevator doors. Jade walked into the hallway and looked first to the left and then the right. When she spotted them, she walked toward them, her slim figure hidden completely in black slacks and sweater. "Damn, Jeff. No wonder you are in love with her. She's beautiful."

Jeff glared at Phil. "She's a wonderful person too. We've got to beat this thing. It will kill her if this lawsuit is successful. I'll never get her if it is."

Phil watched Jeff's face as Jade walked toward them. "So much for keeping your feelings hidden. Your heart is hanging off your sleeve. Let's get this over with."

Jade walked up to them. "Good afternoon."

"Hello, Jade," Jeff greeted her.

"Ms. Kennedy." Phil held out his hand, and she took it briefly. "LeRoy is waiting for us."

Two hours later, Jeff and Jade walked out of the attorney's office, leaving Phil and LeRoy still talking about the case. "Would you like some coffee," he asked.

"Don't be ridiculous. We're already in about as much trouble as we can get. I can't be seen with you again." Tears filled her eyes. "My whole career is on the line because of this. If Penny wins this case, I'll never be able to hold my head up around here again. It's best if we don't try to see each other. I think Phil and LeRoy will agree with that."

"I'm sure they will. I hate this, Jade. I'm sorry you are being dragged into the whole mess. Please call me on the phone if you can't deal with this. I understand your reluctance to be seen with me, but I would still like to talk to you."

She looked at him for a long time. *Don't let him see that you want to step into his arms right this minute. Don't let him guess that I love him as much as he says he loves me. Give me the strength to stay away from him, Lord. Give me courage, please, please, please.* "I'm sure that wouldn't be the best thing, Jeff. We have to stay away from each other. Goodbye. I'll wait for LeRoy to call me about the proceedings. Good luck to all of us. This is going to be hell."

She turned and walked back to the elevators without looking back. Jeff watched her go, his heart full of pain. He turned and took the stairs down to street level in order to avoid her again. As he stepped out into the early darkness of the late winter afternoon, his heart was as cold as the wind that played with his overcoat hem.

A week went by. Jade kept busy with classes and Tommy's rehabilitation until she could stand it no longer. She called Jeff. "Hello," he answered. She was surprised at the coldness in his voice until he realized it was her.

"Dr. Davidson, this is Jade Kennedy."

He sat up straight and whispered, "Jade? Is that really you?"

She noted the obvious distress in his voice. "Yes, I... uh, I haven't heard a word on anything. Can you tell me what's going on, please?"

"Not much, Jade. Phil tells me that LeRoy has been going around the hospital, interviewing everyone he can find about the situation. He's confident that we will be able to get out of the discrimination and other student complaints. The sexual harassment and alienation are the ones that will be the hardest to prove."

"Do you think he can?"

She heard his sigh before he answered. "He has to. If there is any justice at all, he has to."

"I hope so. Well, thanks for the information. Please let me know if anything changes."

"Jade?"

"Yes?"

"What is going on with Tommy?"

"We have a hearing next month to see if we have to go to trial. The students are fighting with everything they can find. I'm spread a little thin right now. With two lawsuits, a recovering child, and classes, it's about all I can take. I sometimes think I won't make it." He thought he could hear tears in her voice as she sniffed.

"You will, Jade. You have to for Tommy's sake. I feel about like you do. Penny is blabbing all over the hospital. Denying any of her allegations only makes it worse. Please don't give up on me. Give us a chance."

She paused for a long time. "I can't, Jeff. Not now."

"Someday?"

"I don't know. This is all so overwhelming. I just don't know. Goodbye." He heard the click of the disconnection. He thought his heart broke with the click. Slowly, he hung up. He sat staring out the window, seeing nothing, for a long time.

Three times in the next month, their case came up for hearing. Three times it was delayed. Jade's nerves were frayed by the snide insinuations by people who did not know her and the endless indecision of waiting. Jeff honored her request to avoid her as much as possible. She lost five pounds she could not afford to lose. Her eyes had permanent dark circles, and she seemed terribly, terribly sad whenever he saw her.

Jeff's disposition took a turn for the worse. He approached Maggie every few days. Their conversation was nearly always the same, "Have you seen her? How is she? Do you think she will see me?"

Maggie's cryptic "yes, fine, and no," remained the same. Jeff was frantic for action. The time dragged slowly toward spring and graduation.

Phil came to his office one day in late April. "Can you keep Penny from graduating if there are further delays?"

"Of course, I don't think she can continue in the program anyway. Her grades and coursework don't warrant her continuing in any case. I have a copy of a paper that was pure plagiarism. That's enough to get her expelled. At least that record is nonnegotiable. She's done here. She'll never graduate if she stays here."

"I hear she is bragging that if there is one more delay, she'll have her degree, and then she won't have to work because she'll have enough to live a life of ease when this is settled."

"Can't LeRoy find anything that will get this over with?"

"We are asking for a hearing next Wednesday. He thinks the judge is tired of delays by her attorney. Keep your fingers crossed that it will be next week."

"Can I tell Jade?"

"No, not yet. It's not that sure."

Jeff watched him walk away. Maggie came up beside him. "Any progress, Doctor?"

"It doesn't sound like it. I just wish this would be over with. I don't think I can stand much more of this."

"Hang in there. I keep praying that it will be all right."

He gave her a slight smile. "That's the last resort, Maggie. Maybe that will work."

Even though he had anticipated something happening, he was not prepared for a Monday call telling him to appear in court on Wednesday morning at nine o'clock.

"Can I call Jade?"

"No, LeRoy will take care of that if we need her." Depressed, he hung up and started planning what to wear to court. *If it weren't for Jade, I think I would give up on this whole thing and put in for a new job somewhere else. With my credentials, I should be able to get something, maybe nothing as good as this but something.*

Chapter 24

Wednesday came. Jeff dressed in his best gray suit, white shirt, and navy tie to appear in court. When he arrived, he saw that Penny was sitting on the front row. She was dressed in a conservative black dress with little jewelry. Jeff thought it made her look sallow and ugly. He assumed it was to make her appear to be the victim in the case. She wore a smug look on her face when she caught him looking at her. He wanted to smash his fist into that sneer and wipe it off her face. Sick at heart, he wondered exactly where the day would take him. He didn't even react when Jade arrived. She too wore black, but it only enhanced her beauty. He wondered how he had gotten into such a mess.

The chairman of the hospital board called their case. They were sworn in one by one before the proceedings started. Jeff thought he had never hated as much as he did when he looked at Penny. He remembered the intern from the year before and felt great pity for the poor guy.

Jeff only remembered part of the trial. Penny made a good case of their socalled romance and how it had progressed to a closeness that had never been. She outlined dates and times when Jade had been in his office or in Tommy's room with Jeff. Jeff was incredulous. *She has notes of every time Jade and he were together. She's a stalker. He* listened as she described seeing Jade in his arms the night Tommy came out of his coma. She told of being run down by Jade as she left his office in a hurry. Penny outlined the times he and Jade had been going over research materials and the night they had been making calls about the lawsuit. She even had information on seeing them in the hall of the law building when they had dealt with Jade's other lawsuit. He burned with anger when she described how she had seen the two of them in each other's arms outside the law library. He hated the way it made them look guilty. They had tried so hard to stay away from each other, and Penny was making it sound disgusting. He wondered what it would take to file a stalking suit against her.

Penny managed to create a few real tears. Jeff had seen liars before but never one so convincing as Penny Hansen. Listening to her presentation and the answers to the questions by her attorney left him feeling sick inside. He was convinced that his career was over and no institution would ever hire him again. When she began to present Jade as the criminal who stole his affections, it was all he could do to sit in the chair. He had never wanted to smash someone in the face before, but he felt he could have killed Penny willingly. The chairman even looked sympathetically toward Penny as she dabbed at her tearless eyes. He wrote a quick note to his attorney. "They are making it sound convincing. What do we do?" His attorney looked at the note. He wrote so called, "Nothing." Jeff almost blew up. How could they sit there and do nothing?

When it was the university attorney's turn, Jeff found himself losing hope. Everything they presented seemed like the famous hearsay evidence he had often heard on TV court programs. She was listing times and dates, but they all seemed to make Penny's case all the more believable. He was feeling lost and angry when the question came up, "Do you have any further witnesses?"

"Yes, Mr. Chairman. We would like to call Margaret Hill to the stand." Jeff looked at his lawyer with questions in his eyes.

"Mrs. Hill, are you familiar with the situation we are discussing?"

"Yes."

"Please feel free to tell us what you know about the case."

"I work the seven-to-three shift in Pediatrics, so I am stationed directly across from Dr. Davidson's office. There isn't much going on there that I do not see. I have listened to the prior testimony. The first night Ms. Hansen claims to have seen Jade Kennedy in Dr. Davidson's arms was the night that her son came out of a two-year coma. She had fainted and the doctor caught her and treated her before she came to. The second incident was when Dr. Davidson, as her mentor for a research paper, met in his office to discuss the work. Ms. Hansen often hung around the doctor's office and was bumped by Jade when she left the doctor's office following a meeting. Student nurses are known for being in a hurry all the time. I have seen numerous ones bump into someone. It happens all the time. I talked with Jade after she left his office. There simply was no time for illicit behavior. The third incident happened when they spent time in the office making phone calls concerning a legal matter." Jeff thought Maggie was doing a magnificent job of defending him.

"On the fourth occasion Ms. Hansen refers to, Dr. Davidson and Jade Kennedy were discussing this lawsuit on the phone in his office. The last incident was in the law building with a number of witnesses, none of which considered anything there to be out of line. I have become good friends of Dr. Davidson. At no time have I seen any relationship between him and Ms. Hansen, nor have I seen any out-of-the-way behavior between the doctor and Jade Kennedy. It is my opinion that we have a jealous woman who is known for creating problems for men who turn down her advances. I would recommend that this committee drop all charges against Dr. Davidson and proceed with the dismissal of Ms. Hansen."

The panel whispered among themselves as the chairman dismissed Maggie. "Do you have further witnesses?"

"Yes, sir. We would like to present the remaining students in the class of 2018. They have evidence that we will all be interested in." Jeff was shocked when all of the students from his ethics class appeared, filing in one after the other, until the room was overflowing and people were lined up along the wall. He didn't dare turn to look at Jade. He was afraid of what he would see in her eyes.

One by one, several were called to the stand. The first two questions were asked of each of them. "Did you ever see anything that would indicate that Dr. Davidson and Miss Penny Hansen were romantically involved or that sexual harassment was involved? And did you ever see anything that would indicate that Dr. Davidson and Jade

Kennedy-Barnes were romantically involved?" Again they all answered no.

Finally, LeRoy asked, "Do you believe that Miss Hansen should become a member of the nursing profession?"

The answers to all the questions were again no. Seventeen people testified that they had not seen any such involvement. Eight students testified that Penny Hansen was incompetent to be a nurse. They offered details of her neglect and idleness during her shifts. They told of finding her asleep during her shifts or dumping the work on others. Jeff's attorney provided adequate paperwork and grade reports to support the third question. Her plagiarized paper was presented. Finally, the board was excused to make their decision.

In the hallway, Jeff waited. He stood off by himself. Jade stood with Phil and LeRoy, waiting for the verdict to come through. Penny, her attorneys, and a heavyset older man waited at the far end of the hall.

All were surprised when fifteen minutes later, the board returned to the session. Jeff feared the decision. It had been such a short time. He was afraid the decision was not going to be in his favor. Jeff was relieved and surprised to hear the "not guilty" verdict come so quickly. He walked out of the courtroom with the weight lifted from his heart, still a little dazed that it had happened so fast. He looked around for Jade but did not see her in the crowd of well-wishing students and faculty that approached him from every side.

His attorneys gave him the final papers and turned him loose. Penny Hansen stormed out of the courtroom after her attorney. All knew it was only a matter of hours before she would be expelled from the program and sent home. Every one of her classmates was happy to see her go. One attorney commented, "Well, for once, the good guys won a suit like this."

Penny was disappearing down the corridor with the strange man by her side. Jeff heard her saying, "But, Daddy, I wanted—"

The man cut her off. Jeff could hear anger in his voice as he attacked Penny. "Don't be stupid, Penny. A man like that is not for you. Now you can move home and find a job. I'm tired of coddling you. Now that your mother is gone, I'm done spoiling you, and I'm done paying for any more of your frivolous lawsuits. I wonder if that young intern last year ever made a pass at you as you claimed or if you made it all up out of spite. How could you do something like that to good people?" Jeff could hear her father berating her as they walked down the hall.

On the following day, Penny Hansen was dismissed from the nursing program and from the university. There was no sympathy given as the Dean stamped the papers that expelled her from the school. Reasons were given on the paperwork, inadequate scholarship and dereliction of duties, dire comments that would keep her out of the nursing field forever. She left campus the next afternoon, bitter and angry at the world.

Word came back a month later that she had married a boy from her hometown after telling everyone that nursing wasn't for her and that she had finally realized that Freddie was waiting for her at home. He worked on air conditioners and heating systems and made adequate money. Many felt it would never be enough for Penny.

Chapter 25

Jeff took two days off after the trial. He stayed home and puttered in his yard, visited with John and Wilma, and played with Tommy for hours on end.

Jade was not mentioned the entire time. When he could stand it no longer, he asked Wilma, "Have you heard any more on the custody suit?"

"Yes, there will be a hearing next week."

"How is Jade taking it?"

"Not well. I'm worried about her, Jeff. She's running on pure nerve, and she's pushing herself so hard. I think she is trying to keep her mind off the allegations the Barneses are making. It did help that your lawsuit turned out in your favor."

"Do you think she would mind if I came to the hearing?"

"I don't think so. I'm surprised that someone doesn't contact you to testify for her."

"Maybe they heard about the other lawsuit," he said bitterly. "I would be glad to testify for her anytime."

The next day, he was contacted by Dr. Black to be available to testify if he was needed. He was glad to be asked so he could have an excuse to appear.

Jeff and Maggie arrived at the courtroom at the same time. They chose seats together. Jeff sat through the preliminary procedures, watching Jade and her senior student lawyers. In spite of his confidence in Dr. Black, he worried as he watched the two young men and one girl prepare to defend Jade. They looked as nervous as he felt.

Jade sat at the small conference table surrounded by her representatives. Even though there were four of them and a large number watching from the audience, she still looked so alone. He wanted to scream at them, "Someone...anyone, do something to take away her stricken look." Her neat black dress only brought out the beauty of her flawless skin. He had never felt so helpless in his life.

The Barneses sat with two lawyers waiting for the hearing to begin. Their expensive clothes screamed money. Clarice had cruel eyes, and Harold appeared to be a man used to having his own way. Jeff listened to their lawyer start explaining their case.

"Your Honor, I represent these grieving grandparents who are asking for custody of the minor child known as Thomas James Barnes. He is the five-yearold son of their only son who was tragically killed in an automobile accident three years ago. The child is their only living grandchild. They are fully prepared to provide everything the boy could want or need. The mother is a poor student with limited resources and massive debts. She is unstable and unfit to raise this child. We are asking that you approve of full custody of the minor child to his grandparents."

Jade sat perfectly still, listening to the accusations. Her lawyers had advised her to keep calm throughout the proceedings. As she listened to the speech by the Barneses lawyers, it was all she could do to hold down her fear. She wanted to jump up and scream at them all: the Barneses, the lawyers, and the judge.

She barely heard the head legal representative stand up in her defense. She became aware that he was present- ing the information concerning the financial assistance the Barneses had withheld for the funeral and medical expenses. He told of the one visit and the comment that the child would be an unwanted vegetable and presented the infor- mation on the second visit after Tommy regained full con- sciousness. He defended Jade's choices for Tommy's care, both during and after his hospitalization. Professor Black explained the current living conditions provided by Jade and her parents. He concluded with "Your Honor, there are no legal or moral grounds for granting these grandparents custody of Tommy Barnes. Kathleen Jade Kennedy-Barnes has successfully protected her child for all of these months. We are asking that you leave the child with his mother on a permanent basis, that the Barneses pay all expenses of this lawsuit and that they contribute to the future education of the child." Jade sat flabbergasted as Dr. Black spoke.

They had warned Jade that the judge might ask for a recess to make a decision. She was very surprised when the judge gazed around the courtroom, looking first at the Barneses and then at Jade. He pulled his silly half-glasses down on his nose and spoke, "I find this a frivolous law- suit." He looked straight at the shocked grandparents. "All evidence indicates that this young woman has done an exceptional job of caring for her child under extenuating circumstances." He stopped and looked directly at Harold Barnes. "I find the records of your lack of support and your negligence to the child until he returned to consciousness to be evidence that you cannot provide emotionally for this boy as well as his mother. I thereby grant full custody of Thomas James Barnes to his mother, Kathleen Jade Kennedy. I would advise Ms. Kennedy that it will be entirely up to her if she wishes to allow visitation by the grandparents with the child. All court costs associated with this hearing will be charged to the Barneses, including the lawyer's fees for Ms. Kennedy, and I would strongly suggest that the grandparents set up a trust fund for the child's education costs." The judge banged his gavel on the desk, gathered his paperwork, and left the podium.

The Barneses sat stunned while their lawyer rushed over to the table where Jade remained sitting. "Can my clients make arrangements to see the boy? You know they have the legal right because the father is dead. Iowa law says that, you know."

Jade stared at him. *Of all the nerve, how dare they want to see Tommy now?* She sighed. "Not now. Perhaps sometime this summer I will allow it if my parents can supervise the visit. For now, just leave us alone."

Jeff, Maggie, and Lori hurried forward to congratulate Jade. Her hands shook as she embraced the two women. "I can never thank you enough for being here for me. I know I will sleep better tonight." She turned to Jeff. "I thank you too, Jeff. It seems that we have both come out of our lawsuits smelling like roses. Now I have only two weeks left before graduation and way too many assignments to complete."

She called me Jeff. She actually called me Jeff. Elated, he asked the three women, "May I treat you all to lunch to celebrate? I think we need to celebrate before we all go back to work."

"That's good of you, Jeff. I'd like that, as long as we all go," Jade told him. "I need to celebrate for a change. Let me call Mom and tell her the verdict before we go. They are waiting to hear what happened."

Jeff was delighted that Jade had agreed to have lunch with them. The four went to one of the upscale restaurants in a nearby hotel. They were all relieved by the judge's verdict.

The other two women kept the conversation going during the meal. He could see that Jade was very relieved. She began to relax and laugh with them as they reviewed the comments made by the nurses. He hadn't seen her laughing for a long time. Two hours later, they separated to go their respective jobs, all with a lighter heart.

"Did you see the look on Clarice's face when Maggie was talking?" Lisa asked. "I thought she was going to have a stroke. Harold didn't seem quite so sorry about the verdict."

Chapter 26

Jeff returned to work on a Monday and threw himself into the end of semester work. His pupils had nothing but good to say about Jade's earlier lectures. He sent her a formal letter of thanks and signed a check much larger than most students had seen in their lives. He wanted to take it to Jade personally but decided against it. She still insisted that they keep their distance. He was afraid she would not see him. In fact, he was afraid she would never see him again.

He kept his word to leave her alone for the rest of the semester. He only heard about her progress from her parents. Tommy became the main joy in his life. He knew he should not get so attached to the child, but as each day brought new achievements from the little boy, he fell more and more in love with him.

Many times, he wanted to plan an activity and invite Jade, but he restrained himself. He hated to admit just how much the trial and the accusations had taken out of him. He promised himself that he would attend the graduation, not because faculty was expected to attend but because he wanted to see Jade receive her coveted diploma.

He was in the backyard talking to John when Jade came home one afternoon just before graduation weekend. They greeted each other warily. "I hear you are graduating next weekend. May I add my congratulations?" Jeff asked her.

"Of course. Now I think I would like to play with Tommy on that swing. I wonder if the swing will hold someone as big as me."

"Come on, and we'll find out," Jeff yelled after her. "You sit, and I'll push."

"Wonderful," she said as she seated herself in the swing. "I haven't been in a swing since I was a kid."

Jeff pushed her. As she began to swing, her hair spread out behind her in the wind. Tommy encouraged her from his seat in the smaller swing with a seat rather than a flat board. Jeff moved from one to another, keeping them both swinging.

Jade laughed, a wonderful sound. Tommy squealed "Again. Again," as Jeff kept pushing them higher and higher.

Soon the three of them were breathless from the exertion. Jade screamed "Enough!" when she almost fell off her seat. Tommy continued to giggle as Jade picked him up and carried him to the slide. "Thanks, Jeff. That was fun. I don't know when I've had so much fun."

"It's good to see you laughing again," he told her.

"It's good to be laughing again. Once the two lawsuits were settled in our favor and I finished all of my class work, I began to feel free for the first time in years."

"It's been a pretty rough time for you, hasn't it?" he asked as they followed Tommy back across the yard where he was begging to go down the slide.

A faraway look came into her eyes as she recalled events from the past six years. "Yes, I suppose it has been hard, but

I knew I could do it if I just kept going. There were a few times I wasn't sure I was going to make it, but here I am, about to graduate and go out into the world. I don't mind admitting, I'm pretty proud that I made it."

Wilma came out of the house with a large tray with sandwiches and iced tea. "Let's have a picnic," she called as she set the tray on the picnic table on Jeff's patio. "Sit down, Jeff. I have more than enough here for all of us, and there are chocolate-chip bars on the table. I'll get them when the sandwiches are gone."

The four of them chatted amiably as Tommy ate his sandwich before climbing down from Jade's lap to play in the sandbox. As they watched him, Jeff turned to Jade, "He's doing remarkably well. I can't believe how rapidly he is catching up. Are you going to be ready to put him in preschool in the fall?"

"Pre-school. I had never thought that far ahead. Do you think he will be ready? That's a big step for him. I haven't taken him anywhere there are other little children. I don't know how he would do in a classroom with normal kids."

"As fast as he's catching up, he should be fine. There is a special school across from the hospital. They take medically fragile kids year-round, but I've heard they have a summer school program. I'll be glad to look into it for you and give them a recommendation if that is what you want to do."

"I'll have to think about it." She sat for a long time, watching Tommy play. "Please, go ahead and see if he can get in that program. He'll be way behind the rest, but he is almost six. I think I want to see him a year in something like that rather than trying to send him straight to kindergarten."

They continued to watch Tommy. Jeff finally asked, "Jade, would you mind if I come to your graduation ceremonies? I'd really like to see you get your diploma."

She smiled at him. "Mind? Of course not, I'd be happy to have you there." He left a few minutes later to go back to the big empty house. He was elated to think that she had actually smiled and agreed that he could come to her milestone day.

The final two weeks of Jade's program flew by. She said goodbye to all of the people in Geriatrics before going down to Pediatrics to visit with Maggie and Lisa. "The big day is coming," she told them. "I have my cap and gown all ready. Are you guys coming?"

"I wouldn't miss it for the world," Maggie told her. "I feel that I'm partly responsible for you reaching this goal. Have you thought of a job?"

"Yes, I applied with the hospital in Obstetrics. I think I liked that rotation the best of them all next to Pediatrics. I would apply for Pediatrics, but I don't think I want to be that close to Jeff."

"Oh, Jade. I thought you two were getting along a lot better. You worked pretty well together in ER. You could work well up here too."

"I just hope the hospital will put me somewhere, either on a day or afternoon shift. I'd like to be available to take care of Tommy at night. My folks do a great job during the day. I know they wouldn't mind if I worked nights, but I don't want to be sleeping all day while Tommy's awake. Did I tell you that I am going to enroll Tommy in the special school for the summer? They will see if he is ready for kindergarten in the fall. Just think, Maggie. He may start school just like every other kid."

"Oh, honey, I hope so. That would be wonderful for you if he can."

Chapter 27

Graduation day arrived with perfect spring weather. The crab apples and ornamental pear trees were blooming all along the university drives as Jeff drove the Kennedys and Tommy to the auditorium where the nurses were receiving their diplomas. To everyone's delight, Jade had been chosen to play the Dvorak Symphony as the entertainment for the ceremony. He closed his eyes and allowed himself to drift with the lovely melody. Sadness filled him during the River Road section. He wondered where the roads would lead him in the next few months.

He thought about the two offers sitting on his desk to move to other states and head up new Pediatric surgical departments. He knew it would all hinge on Jade's behavior toward him after the ceremony. He didn't think he could manage to stay around if she scorned him. He joined them in heartfelt clapping when Jade walked across the stage and took the precious document in her hand.

John, Wilma, Tommy, and Jeff stood waiting outside the auditorium as Jade wound her way through the crowd toward them. Tommy waved to her from atop Jeff's broad shoulders. Her face lit up when she saw them waiting there. She flashed him one of her fabulous smiles as she accepted hugs and congratulations from her parents, hugged Tommy, and then turned to Jeff. "Jeff, I want to thank you for all you have done to help me get Tommy and my career in nursing going. In case you have forgotten, we have some things to discuss now that I have safely graduated. Now that I'm free of the student-faculty bans, I have a few things to discuss with you."

His face lit up with delight. "Does that mean you will go out with me? Can I tell you I love you and want you to be my wife?"

"Yes, you certainly can. And now I am free to tell you I love you too and to finally hug you." She laughed with delight as she pulled away from him. "Unless you are involved in the Pediatric psychiatric master's program."

He hugged her tight against him, hoping she knew that he never wanted to let her go. "No, that's Dr. Anderson's realm, not mine."

"Do you object to me enrolling this fall?"

"No way. Would you please answer my question while I have these witnesses to help me hold you to your answer?"

"Of course, I'll marry you sometime this summer and go back to school this fall. I would like for Mom and Dad to live here in the guesthouse for a while at least. After that, they can travel as they intended, and we can hire a student gardener."

"They can stay forever, for all I care. Keep the guesthouse for them between trips." He gave her a big hug, overwhelmed to be holding her willingly in his arms. A group of her fellow students walking by gave wolf whistles and encouraging comments to the couple. Although he was a bit hesitant, she offered no resistance to his caress.

"We have a lot of plans to make then," she told him as they broke apart and headed for the car. "Maggie and Lori are waiting right over there to help us." They turned and waved at their friends. Tommy giggled and squirmed to be put down. Everyone cheered as he raced across the lawn toward Maggie and "Lowee," screaming happily as he ran.

He stopped and again took her in his arms. "Jade, I've got an idea. What do you think of me adopting Tommy? I'd like us all to have the same name," Jeff asked Jade as they watched him run to his friends.

"Tommy? Tommy Davidson, I think that would be perfect," she answered happily as she pulled him closer and kissed him soundly. Their audience clapped and cheered them on as he took her hand and led her across the lawn for a photo shoot.

Epilogue

Two years later, the same group gathered to cheer for Jade as she received her master's in child psychology. Tommy stood beside John with a big smile on his face. "Look, Gramps, Mom is really doing well."

"So are you, Buddy. Now you are seven and in first grade already. We are pretty proud of all of your accomplishments." John realized that the boy had returned to "normal" for his age. They all thanked God for his progress.

Maggie and Lori stood with their husbands, waiting to greet Jade when she walked toward them with a big smile on her face and a rolled sheepskin in her hand. A gold cord hung around her neck.

Jeff beamed at his wife as she came toward them. The tiny three-month-old baby girl wriggled in his arms before letting out a huge yawn just as Jade approached them. He shifted the baby to one arm, reached for Jade with his other and pulled her to him. "Congratulations, sweetheart. We're so proud of you."

Jade kissed him, touched the little girl's head, and reached out to hug Tommy. "It was perfect, Jeff. I'm so happy." They stood together, chatting with the little group of family and friends. As they turned to walk to their car thirty minutes later, Wilma was not at all surprised to hear Jade say to Jeff, "Have you heard that the doctorate program in child psychology starts in two months. What would you think if I…"

About the Author

Been there, done that! Lois Lamb was raised on an Iowa farm. Following a divorce, she worked at anything to make a buck to keep her three and four other teenagers going. She has experience designing kitchens, dispatching telephone repair crews, medical insurance filing, activity leader in a nursing home, secretary, semi-truck weigher, house cleaner, dorm supervisor at a National Park, restaurant cook and hostess, Cancer Research Field person, special librarian and customer service representative. Along the way, Lois traveled to Europe, herded wild horses in Nevada, lived on a cattle ranch in Oklahoma for six years and pursued hobbies in painting, portraiture and quilting. Through it all, she wrote, wrote, wrote. Lois Lamb has a BLS degree from the University of Iowa, a BSE in Secondary English from NWMo State University and a Master's degree in Library and Information Science from the University of Iowa. Her goal is to teach women and show them they can succeed under whatever circumstances they may face. Lois Lamb currently lives in Clear Lake IA with her husband, Nathan.